Bad Influence

Bad Influence

WILLIAM SUTCLIFFE

HAMISH HAMILTON
an imprint of
PENGUIN BOOKS

HAMISH HAMILTON

Published by the Penguin Group
Penguin Books Ltd, 80 Strand, London WC2R ORL, England
Penguin Group (USA), Inc., 375 Hudson Street, New York, New York 10014, USA
Penguin Books Australia Ltd, 250 Camberwell Road, Camberwell, Victoria 3124, Australia
Penguin Books Canada Ltd, 10 Alcorn Avenue, Toronto, Ontario, Canada M4V 3B2
Penguin Books India (P) Ltd, 11 Community Centre, Panchsheel Park, New Delhi – 110 017, India
Penguin Books (NZ) Ltd, Cnr Rosedale and Airborne Roads, Albany, Auckland, New Zealand
Penguin Books (South Africa) (Pty) Ltd, 24 Sturdee Avenue, Rosebank 2196, South Africa

Penguin Books Ltd, Registered Offices: 80 Strand, London WC2R ORL, England

www.penguin.com

First published 2004
2

Set in 11/13 pt Monotype Dante
Typeset by Rowland Phototypesetting Ltd,
Bury St Edmunds, Suffolk
Printed in Great Britain by Clays Ltd, St Ives plc

A CIP catalogue record for this book is available from the British Library

ISBN 0–241–14140–0

For Maggie

my house

I know what it is you want. You want to know who's to blame. You're trying to figure out if any of it was my fault. So here's a new theory for you. It was Olly's aunt's fault. All of it. She started the whole thing. I've never met her, and I don't know where she lives or what she looks like, but that doesn't mean she can't be to blame. If you look at it logically, she's the one you should be going after.

On the day it began, she got ill. Or maybe it was divorced. Or married. It was something like that anyway, and Olly had to go off, leaving me on my own.

If Olly's aunt hadn't done whatever it is she did that Sunday, Olly wouldn't have gone, and if Olly hadn't gone I never would have met Carl, and if I'd never met Carl, everything would still be OK. I wouldn't know who you are, you wouldn't know who I am, and we'd both be spared your boring, boring visits.

I should have known from his clothes that he was going to be taken away. He's not in jeans, but grey trousers with a crease down the front, and he isn't wearing a T-shirt, but a proper grown-up shirt, buttoned right to the top. It looks wrong with all the buttons done up, and I would have undone the neck if I'd been made to wear it, but Olly isn't very good at figuring out things like that.

He often looks a bit funny, Olly. He has a knack of tucking things in that should hang out, and of doing things up that should be left undone. And he always dresses for two months colder than it really is. Every time he comes round, he leaves at least one jumper behind. When I go over to his, I usually have an armful of clothes to deliver. But I don't mind any of that. It's part of what makes him Olly. The section of his head a more normal person uses thinking about clothes, he uses for strange ideas and facts no one else knows.

'What are you *wearing*?' I ask, when he walks in.

'Check this out,' he says.

Slowly and elaborately, as if it's a magic display, he points to a flap of material he's got on each shoulder. Waving his fingers around like he's showing off to an audience of fifty people, he carefully unbuttons them, one after the other, then he wiggles his shoulders, making the flaps flap.

'You will never,' he says, 'you will *never* guess what these are.'

'Yes, I will,' I say.

'Go on, then,' he says.

'They're flaps,' I say.

'Wrong!' he says, hitting the word like a bell.

'It's not wrong. I can see them. They're flaps.'

'They're more than flaps,' he says, narrowing his eyes to try and look mysterious.

I never fall for his mysterious look, especially not when he's wearing a shirt buttoned all the way to the top with stupid flaps sticking out from his shoulders, so I say nothing and cross my arms to show I'm not impressed.

'They're hat flaps,' he says.

'Cat flaps?'

'Hat flaps. Flaps for hats. For soldiers' hats. In the navy. If it was green, instead of yellow, it'd be a proper uniform.'

'Don't be an idiot,' I say. 'They don't have soldiers in the navy. They have sailors. And they don't wear green. They wear navy. That's why navy's called navy.'

'No, it isn't. If navy was navy because of the navy, green wouldn't be green. Green would be army.'

Talking to Olly is like swimming. At any moment you might just sink.

There's an owl on the floor of my bedroom that isn't really an owl any more. I made it at school, and originally it had eyes and nose and mouth and feet, but even then it looked more like a football than an owl, so it got kicked around all the time, and first the feet fell off, then the nose, then the mouth, then one eye. Now it's just a football with an eye, but I still call it Owl.

I pick it up, wedge it under one of Olly's hat flaps, and do up the button. Olly watches, all cross-eyed because it's too close for him to see. Owl's just the right size, so I get a bear from the back of my cupboard and button it under the other flap.

We walk to the bathroom so Olly can see, and he looks a total idiot, but he seems to like it, and we run all over the house doing different moves to see if the owl and the bear will fall out, but whatever we do, they just stay there, jiggling around. After a while, the running around turns into other things, and we end up playing the game where I chuck Cluedo men up from the patio and Olly tries to catch them from the bedroom window, and he almost falls out, which is really funny. After that Olly chickens out, so we start a proper game of Cluedo, and all along he's still wearing the animals. I can't even tell if he still realizes.

I bet you think you know all about Olly, but you don't. There's nothing wrong with him. If I was given the chance again, I'd still want him to be my best friend, exactly how things were.

When you've got a best friend, you don't need anything else in the world. It's like armour, or one of those force-fields you get on computer games that make a wailing sound, and you glow orange and, for as long as you're orange, bullets and missiles just bounce off you.

Olly's been my best friend for so long, I don't even notice the force-field any more because it's become permanent. When he goes off, it's like a layer of me has been peeled away. I don't know what to do. I can't settle. Even if I'm busy, or having fun, in my head I'll be imagining telling Olly about it later.

Once, when I was trying to phone home to get picked up, I rang Olly's house by mistake, and I had to tell his mum it was a wrong number. She thought I was mad. It happened without me thinking.

By the time his mum arrives to take him off to his aunt's, I've still not got round to asking why he's dressed up, so I'm totally unprepared for him being whisked away. There's no warning or anything. It's like someone walking in and confiscating your legs.

It's not really like that. If someone pulled your legs off, you'd bleed to death.

She doesn't ask Olly why he's wearing an owl and a bear on his shoulders, she just pulls them out and leaves them by the front door. I was hoping he'd walk out with them still on, which he almost does.

When the door closes behind him, I look at my watch, and there's still the whole of Sunday afternoon to go.

You wouldn't think it'd make much difference that it's a Sunday when it's the holidays anyway, but it does. Everyone's about. The house always feels too full on a Sunday, but also

4

too empty. If you want the telly, or the kitchen table, or the sunny bit of lawn, chances are someone will have got there first. But even though all the good bits of the house are taken, I sometimes feel as though my family are just wandering about, lost, without any real idea of what to do with themselves until the day's over and everything can return to normal on Monday. It's as if Sunday always takes them by surprise, as if each week they don't quite believe it's going to happen, then it does and they're not prepared and all they can do is stagger around waiting for it to be over.

For hours I'm good, and I look after myself and do stuff in my room. I even try to finish off our game of Cluedo on my own, but it doesn't work, and I end up cheating to find out who did the murder. It's Professor Plum, which is unusual. Playing a board game on your own is like talking to yourself. You're embarrassed in case someone comes in and finds you doing it. Also, it's no fun.

Eventually I have to go and annoy Donny.

donny's room

There are two 'Keep Out' signs on the door. Between them is an orange sticker showing three black oblongs with wobbly lines of steam rising from them, stamped with a big red cross. Underneath the steaming oblongs it says: 'DANGER: HAZARDOUS WASTE'.

There's a knack to getting the door open without being heard. Just as the handle goes past the slack bit, you give it a sharp pull towards you, while pressing a toe against the bottom corner that always sticks.

Q: Why am I expending energy opening the door silently when I know he's in there?
A: Because those first few unobserved seconds can give a critical advantage.

I take a breather when I've got the door free of the latch. That's the hardest bit. So far, the operation is a complete success. No squeak, click, thump or scrape to give me away.

I poke my nose through the gap. The skilful spy uses all five senses for the gathering of intelligence. Any early information could prove useful. I set my nasal lab team to work on the first waft.

An interesting thing's happened to the smell of Donny's room recently. It's like what happens to cheese. First it smells nice, then it smells a bit funny but you still don't mind eating it, then something amazing happens, and suddenly you open

6

up the fridge and think, 'Oh my God! Something's died in here!'

My theory is that Boy Room Pong follows a cheese pattern (see fig. 1).

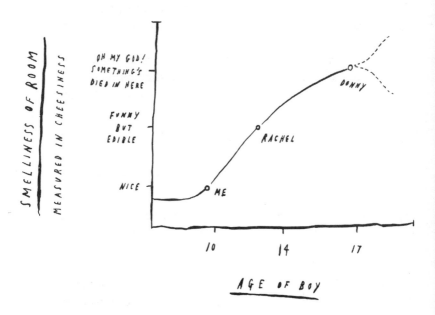

FIGURE 1. BOY ROOM PONG

SMELLINESS OF ROOM

MEASURED IN CHEESINESS

OH MY GOD! SOMETHING'S DIED IN HERE

FUNNY BUT EDIBLE

NICE

ME

RACHEL

DONNY

10 14 17

AGE OF BOY

IMPORTANT NOTE: RACHEL IS NOT A BOY AND THEREFORE HAS NO PLACE ON THIS DIAGRAM. SHE IS INCLUDED FOR INFORMATION ONLY.

As you can see from the graph, there are two theories of what the future holds for the Donny Room Pong. I favour the up-then-down curve, since I don't think a room could smell worse and still sustain human life. The DRP is probably at its peak right now. But who knows? Maybe it'll just go up and up, until plastic objects in his room start to melt, and we discover that Donny's an alien who can survive without the need for oxygen.

Today, the DRP is bad, but not so bad that I'll have to abort my mission. It tells me nothing I don't know already: that he's in there, that he's been in there for several hours, and that none of the windows are open.

I open the door a few more centimetres, giving myself a view of half the room. He's at his desk, in the homework crouch. This means one of three things:

a) He is doing his homework.
b) He has assumed the pose having heard the door open.
c) He is gazing blankly out of the window like a total mong, thinking, 'If I hadn't been sitting here for the last two hours, gazing blankly out of the window like a total mong, I'd have finished this by now and would be out having fun.'

My money is on c).

Not that I have any money. It's what you call a turn of phrase.

I've never once got the door more than half open without being seen. Even if they don't hear or see anything, people just know when someone's walked into a room, doubly so if they're Donny because that makes you paranoid and secretive, triply so if the person walking into the room is me because Donny's greatest joy in life is chucking me out of wherever it is I want to be, and quadruply so when Donny's term's already started (ha, ha) and mine hasn't.

This time, all records are smashed. I get the door fully open, all the way to the point where it bonks against the bed if you let it. Donny hasn't heard a thing.

I take a couple of steps into the room on tiptoe. If this had ever happened before, I'd have the locations of all the squeaking floorboards memorized, but there's no precedent for such a brilliant and silent entry. We're in virgin territory here. The history books are being torn up with every step I take.

Five steps later, I'm right behind him. This is *amazing*. If you'd ever tried to get into my brother's room, you'd understand. This is like someone running the 100 metres in *5 seconds*. This is like someone driving a car so fast that it just takes off without even trying.

Today, a great victory for younger brothers all over the globe has been scored. Feel the adulation.

'BOO!' I shout, thinking, this is going to be big. There's no road map for how angry Donny's going to be when he realizes where I am.

But there's nothing. No reaction. He just stays in the homework crouch and doesn't even jump.

I tap him on the shoulder. Still he doesn't twitch or speak.

'Hi,' I say. 'Are you pleased to see me?'

The corpse act continues.

OK, so he's ignoring me. This changes everything. The history books will have to be Sellotaped back together again. He's not reacting, even now, so there's no way of knowing how far I got undetected.

Donny's like that. Just when you think you know where you stand, he'll flip everything upside-down. It does my head in,

9

and sometimes it makes me hate him, but most of all it makes me want to get into his room and think of something to do where I win and he loses.

So this is the state of play: he won the getting-in-undetected game (by a particularly sneaky means), but this has segued into a Donny-ignoring-me challenge which I know I can win because now he's exposed his greatest weakness. He's laid himself completely open.

Q: The weakness?
A: His stuff.

He hates me touching his stuff. Now I'm in his room, and he's facing away from me, and if he turns to look at me he's lost, and I've got a whole room full of Donny's Stuff to pick up and put down at my leisure.

Oh, the moment is sweet.

I look around me, trying to choose where to start. There are piles of tapes and magazines and books on his bedside table. There's also a shelf in the corner, piled with mysterious tubes and bottles and sprays and lotions. So many things to fiddle with and clank and jostle, to open and shut with satisfying clicks, squelches and snaps. And if we're talking untouchables, there's his guitar, propped up against the wall, just begging for a big, fat, noisy strum.

Then there's the holy of holies – the total exclusion zone – the drawer in his bedside table. God knows what's in there. Normally, Donny twitches if you so much as look at it. Now I'm blatantly staring at the drawer, and nothing's happening because Donny's trapped himself into ignoring me.

Victory will come at a price. I know that. The greater the victory, the greater the physical pain he'll inflict on me. Do I dare go for the drawer? Can I risk the reaction that would be provoked by this, the supreme triumph?

Then I think of a whole other avenue. He's trying to play it psychological rather than physical today, and there's a way – yes, there's a brilliant way – to beat him using his own methods. He won't be able to hurt me so much, either. It almost makes me laugh out loud when I think of it.

I pace for a few moments, drawing out the tension, then I go for it. I clatter a couple of tapes together to make it sound like I've picked something up, then I say, 'What's this?'

His head spins round. Yes! Victory!

And there's nothing in my hands!! Double victory! Oh, yyeeeeessssssssssss! The genius of it!

Donny glowers, then turns back to his desk.

This is annoying. I have scored – as any neutral referee would definitely confirm – a great victory, but Donny hasn't done the decent thing and got angry. He hasn't even thrown me out.

Then I notice he's drawing something. I can't quite see what it is. I think it might be a woman, but it's hard to tell because the legs and arms are at funny angles. He's shielding it from me with his body. Suddenly, the piles of stuff that seemed interesting to fiddle with lose all appeal. I want to see what he's drawing. But if I ask to look, I've lost. If I even just go closer and show I'm interested, I've still lost.

When I'm seventeen, I'll know how to be evil, like Donny. He's the ultimate adversary. You can never win.

I turn away and decide to go for broke. There's only one way I can come out of this on top. He's raised the stakes at every turn, and I can't just back down. There's only one place to go now. The bedside table drawer.

I slide it open as quietly as I can. I turn and check, but there's no reaction from Donny. The minute he recognizes the sound of the drawer, he's going to go nuclear. If this happens before I've successfully taken anything out, I reckon that makes it a dead heat, which isn't worth the beating-up I'm going to get.

I can see something blue in there. A lid. The lid of a tub. It's not a square tub, and it's not round, either. I've never seen a tub that shape before. I gently, silently lift it out of the drawer and take a good look. It's a squidged rectangle, about the size of my palm. There's a word on it that I've never seen before.

I open it up, and it's half full of colourless gunge. It looks like glue. I take a sniff, and there's something about the smell that's just not gluey. It's an oily, slippery smell, not a sticky smell. You can see his finger marks in the dent where he's been scooping it out.

'What's this?' I ask.

He doesn't turn or speak. He stays in the crouch, drawing.

'What is it?'

No reaction.

'It smells funny.'

Still nothing.

I take another look at the word on the lid. 'Vaseline,' I say. 'What's it for?'

Suddenly, he's on me. His hand's round my wrist and he's squeezing it till I drop the tub, then he gets me by the trousers and lifts me off the ground, right up to head height, and I'm saying, 'Don't! Don't!', but I'm also laughing because I actually like this bit, and he throws me down as hard as he can on to the bed, and I can tell he's really cross because he throws me right into the corner so my head bangs against the wall. Suddenly I want to leave, but he picks me up again, and I scream as loud as I can, 'Get ooooooooooooooooooooffffffff !', but he chucks me down just as roughly. This time it doesn't hurt because I cover my head, so I get up quickly, faster than he's expecting, and butt him in the stomach, which he isn't prepared for. I dive between his legs, making a dash for it on my knees, but he gets me by the ankle, and pulls me back, and I'm yelling, 'Aaaaaahhhhhh! My faaaaaaaaaaaace!', because I'm getting a massive carpet burn on my cheek. Then he drops my ankle and as soon as my feet slap against the floor, he sits on me and bounces up and down like he's testing my suspension, and he tells me that if I ever go in that drawer again or even come into his room without asking, he'll pull out chunks of my hair until I look like a cancer victim. I don't want him to have the satisfaction of thinking I've heard him, so I just shout, 'VASELINE! VASELINE! VASELINE!', at the top of my voice, then I'm upside-down in mid air, and suddenly I'm flat on my tummy on the landing, and his door's slammed behind me.

My chest aches and my eyes feel bulgy and sore, as if he made them almost pop out.

But it's better than being ignored.

CONCLUSION: A complicated and very technical conflict, with a narrow victory for me, in which a major stronghold was stormed (the bedside drawer), and a new weapon was discovered (the word 'Vaseline').

the kitchen

A man needs a little respite sometimes, so I opt for the kitchen. There's a nice, lemony smell in the air, and a big pot's on the stove, its lid jizzling with the steam that's coming out. Mum's got a pile of chicken thighs in front of her, as if a whole load of chickens have got scared and flown away so fast that they left their legs behind.

She's picking them up one by one, doing something with a knife, then pulling the skin off in a big, gloopy yank. It's really sick and gory, and you can tell it makes the same noise as if you pulled a dead person's skin off, and straight away I know I want a go.

'Can I do one?' I ask.

'If you wash your hands first.'

There's always a catch. This is how Mum gets me out of the kitchen – by demanding weird cleanliness rituals – but this time I'm not going to be such a pushover. I need to know what it feels like to pull skin off. Then I'll be able to tell Olly I pretty much know what it's like to pull someone's face off. Because it's bound to feel the same. Except for the holes where the eyes and mouth are, but I can make that up. So I wash my hands without even complaining and sit down next to Mum.

She makes a slit in the skin, and hands over a chicken leg. It's cold and clammy, and much more leggy than I thought it was going to be. I've only ever touched them when they're cooked, and they're less leggy then. I grip the bone with my left hand

and take a loose flap of skin between my finger and thumb. I give it a pull, but my hands come off the skin before the skin comes off the chicken. It's too slippy.

'You have to grip harder,' says Mum, trying to pretend she's not smiling, but I know she is. She can see I'm not enjoying myself as much as I hoped.

I unwrinkle my nose, to try and show her she's wrong, and grab the skin with all my fingers at once, using my nails for extra grip. I tug hard and, with an amazing ripping sound, the gooey, goose-pimply skin comes away from the meat. It's like tearing someone to bits. It's incredible. And suddenly I've got a dangly, white flap of gloop in one hand and a lump of pink dead thing in the other. I drop both. It's like when you get off a roller-coaster. You feel a bit sick and glad it's over, but also ultra-happy and pleased with yourself.

'You want to do the rest?' asks Mum. She's still got that smile on.

'No, I'm busy.'

I stand up and walk to the door, but I'm hoping she'll say something because I'm not really ready to leave yet.

'Wash your hands,' she says, predictably.

I stop, and shrug.

'Ben, you're covered in raw chicken. Wash your hands, now.'

I lean against the wall. The important thing is that she doesn't think I'm a wimp. She mustn't think I'm running away.

'Can we cut eyes and a mouth into one of the chicken legs?' I ask. 'Then when we skin it we'll know what it feels like to pull someone's face off.'

There's a look you get from Mum when you take her by surprise that has loads of meanings, starting from 'What are you talking about?' going all the way up to 'Who are you?

Surely we're not related.' This one registers pretty high (see fig. 2).

She's stuck for an answer, which feels good. I could leave now, but I can't think of anywhere to go, so I stay in the corner.

Mum carries on skinning the chicken legs.

'Why don't you go and help Dad in the garden?' she says.

I walk to the window and look. He's still slicing up a tree branch with a chainsaw. It's his new toy. He said our neighbour's branch was cutting out all the light from the upstairs – which is totally stupid because even if you close the curtains light still gets in – so he went out and bought a chainsaw and chopped it down. Now he's cutting it up into logs, even though we've only got central heating, so no one knows what he wants logs for. He's funny like that. I think he just wanted the chainsaw.

Even before he took it out of the box he told me I wasn't allowed to touch it, using a specially horrible voice, like he was already cross with me for something I hadn't even done yet. I reckon he wants me to go out and watch, but I'm deliberately not going to, so he knows how unfair it is that I'm not allowed a go.

I don't like Sundays. They're twice as long as other days.

The phone rings, which for some reason makes Mum gasp and stare at her hands, tutting and sighing, as if the phone ringing is a terrible freak event, like a fridge landing on your head when you're out for a walk in the countryside.*

She gets up and leaps at the kitchen-towel holder on the wall, rolls down a sheet with her elbow, and pulls it off using her

* Apparently that happened once, and they died, and no one ever found out whose fridge it was. According to Olly. This is a footnote, which is a place to put extra information at the bottom of the page. I might use more later, but only if I remember.

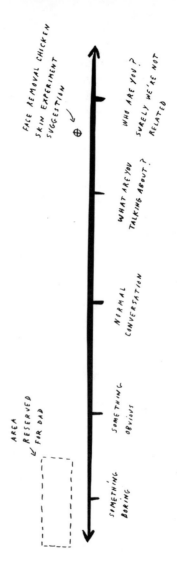

FIGURE 2. THINGS YOU CAN SAY TO MUM

chin for grip. Then she picks up the phone, holding it with the kitchen towel as if it's made of dog poo.

'Hello?' she says, natural as anything, pretending she hasn't got kitchen towel tickling her nose.

There's a long silence – an extra-long silence – during which she mouths at me frantically to wash my hands, but I pretend not to understand.

When Mum eventually speaks, it's to say, 'Oh, noooo. He didn't. Oh, no.'

This means two things:

1) It's Auntie Kath.
2) Mum'll be on the phone for an hour – minimum.

I wander out of the room. The door handle feels weirdly sticky.

I hate Sundays.

rachel's room

I stand in the hall for a bit.

You're not supposed to stand in the hall. The radiator's never on there – I think to encourage people to move on. I don't know why this is so important, but you can tell it is. If Dad had his way, there'd be loud-hailers on the walls programmed to say, 'Move along now, people. There's nothing to see here.'

He hates it when Mum stands in the hall with the door open saying goodbye to someone for longer than they were in the kitchen having tea in the first place. When Dad says goodbye, it takes about half a second.

He's definitely twitchy about the hall. Maybe there's a body under the floorboards. After you're dead, worms and insects eat you except for your bones and teeth, and if the police find your teeth they can tell who you are by asking your dentist where your fillings went. Once they know who you are, they can often tell who killed you, so even after years and years if you've killed someone you're never safe.

The only thing in the hall, apart from the radiators that are always off and the lights that are always on, is a big cupboard with games in it. Even though I know the inside of this cupboard better than I know the inside of any cupboard in the world, I open it up and take a look. Everything's exactly where it always is – even the Fuzzy Felt that hasn't been touched for years, except one evening last summer when Mum and Dad were away and Donny filled the house with his strange friends who never take their hoods down, and they smoked chocolatey-smelling cigarettes and started making weird pictures with Fuzzy Felt circus animals that they thought were really funny.

The cupboard's no help. There's nothing in there I fancy. I open and shut the door a few times, seeing how many different noises it can make, then I decide to go and see what Rachel's up to.

I get all the way to her room without touching the stairs, using just the banister, the skirting board and a few bits of wall. It's easy, really. The banister creaks and sags when you do it. One day it's going to break and I'll plunge to my death, but it doesn't happen this time.

She's in her room. Obviously, Lucy's in there, too. The Lucy–Rachel situation is probably best explained by a Venn diagram (see fig. 3). Donny thinks Lucy's a lesbian, but I reckon that's just his way of saying he fancies her.

There's no point in trying anything clever on the entry front. Rachel doesn't go for that kind of thing. You have to just walk in, as if you're delivering an important message from Mum, then play for time until she realizes you've got no reason to be there, by which point you've hopefully invented one. It's hard to think of one in advance because you never know what's going on in there.

You couldn't draw a diagram of the smells in Rachel's room. Not even a scatter graph. There's no pattern to it at all. Something's always happening, though, and it always makes its own smell, which comes out of one of her zillions of bottles, jars, tubes and sprays. A zillion isn't a real number, it's just a turn of phrase.

Sometimes the Rachelucy smell tickles your nose, sometimes it grabs you by the throat, but whatever it is, however much

FIGURE 3.

VENN DIAGRAM EXPLAINING THE RACHEL/LUCY SITUATION

you first think it might be choking you, it's a smell that always makes you want to stay there longer.

'Hi,' I say, in the tone of voice you'd use if you'd been invited. I take one step into the room.

They both look at me crossly, like I've caught them in the middle of something private. This is how they always look at me.

A quick glance around is enough to tell there's something interesting going on. It looks like the room's been burgled, except by a very fussy burglar who couldn't find anything he liked. There are clothes all over the room, magazines scattered everywhere, and cosmetics, aerosols, tissues and perfumes are heaped on the bed, in a pile so big you could hide in it.

Then I notice how they're dressed. They were in jeans and sweatshirts at lunchtime; now they're wearing strange things on their legs that aren't trousers but aren't really tights either, and their shirts aren't like normal shirts because you can see right through the material to their skin. They're both wearing lacy gloves that stop halfway down the fingers like Madonna's or the milkman's, and their hair's standing up on end like they're skydiving. There are blue lines around their eyes, splodges of red on their cheekbones, and their mouths are smeared with fishy-pink lipstick that twinkles. If they were on TV you'd twiddle your controls to try and get the picture back to normal.

I remember they dressed like this once before when they were getting ready to go to someone's birthday party, and Dad was supposed to be driving them, but he wouldn't do it because he said they looked like whores, and there was a huge argument, and they refused to change, and Rachel had a big hissy, weepy fit, and eventually Mum took them, then when Mum got back from taking them, she and Dad had a huge row that ended with them going to bed really early, and I could hear the bed squeaking from the living room, but I never said anything even though it made me feel sick, and it was obvious what they were doing because they had to get up again later to go and fetch Rachel and Lucy, and it was Dad who went this time and suddenly he didn't seem to mind at all.

'What do you want, nosey shit-nose?' says Rachel.

'Just came to say hi.'

'Hi. Bye.'

'What are you doing?'

'I'm chucking you out of my room.'

'Hi, Lucy.' It's an old tactic. Appeal to a higher authority. Or a different one, anyway.

'Hi, Ben.' There's something friendly in her voice. It's a toehold.

'How are you doing?' I ask. I need to think of something more interesting than that, but my mind's gone blank. She just shrugs.

'You look nice,' I say.

That, it turns out, is all wrong. She scowls and bags out her shirt with her hand, as if she's just remembered it's see-through.

'10, 9, 8, 7 . . .' says Rachel. She doesn't even need to explain what it is she's counting down to these days, but once she starts, you just know you don't want to be in the same room as her when she gets to one.

'I won't be in your way. I'll just sit here.'

'6, 5, 4 . . . Do you want a face full of hairspray?' She picks up an aerosol from the bed, flicks off the lid, and points it at me, her finger poised on the nozzle like a sharpshooter. If I had one, too, we could have a duel. With a match, I could use mine as a flame-thrower. Except that it might explode and blow my whole hand off.

'3, 2 . . .' Her arm straightens, and her finger stiffens. She'll spray. She's got that look in her eye.

'Are you dressing up as whores?' I say.

'1.'

I duck and run for it.

Outside the room I stand there for a bit, thinking.

'Bye, Lucy!' I shout.

A little puff of hairspray comes out through the keyhole.

'That could've blinded me!'

'Shouldn't be looking.' Rachel's voice is muffled through the door.

'I wasn't!'

'Good.'

'But I could've been!'

'Would've taught you a lesson, then.'

'Mum'd kill you if you blinded me.'

'Wouldn't care.'

'Yes, you would.'

'No, I wouldn't.'

'Yes, you would.'

I decide to leave it there, while I'm ahead. Don't want Rachel to think I'm immature.

In Donny's room, it's like a game of chess followed by a round of all-in wrestling against someone twice your size. In Rachel's room, it's like diving without knowing how far away the water's going to be. You just jump off and wait for the splash.

The other upstairs room is Mum and Dad's. I wander in, but not to see what there is because it's always the same. There's never anything to see in Mum and Dad's room. The point is their window, a big, curvy one that gives you a view of the street in both directions. Because you're upstairs, no one knows you're looking at them. If I'm really bored, I'll go in there to see if anything's happening in the street, even though nothing ever is. It's not a dead end, but our street isn't on the way to anywhere, so usually it's empty.

The flats at the bottom end got turned into a nuthouse, and once a day the mad people who live there are herded up and down the street a few times, but once you're used to them it's not funny any more. Mrs Hale from down the road organized a campaign to stop it happening. Mum wouldn't join in, and now when they see each other they both pretend the other one's invisible. Donny used to be able to make me cry by pretending I was invisible, but that was years ago.

When you've run out of options, checking to see what's going on in the street is your last hope.

This time, it's a miracle. Something is happening. There's a boy in a red tracksuit. A boy I don't recognize. He looks about my age, maybe a bit older, and it doesn't seem like he's just passing through. He's standing there, diagonally opposite, with a ball. He's chucking it downwards as hard as he can and seeing how high it bounces.

The answer is: high. He's not bad. And it looks like a good ball. Rubber. I can tell from where I'm standing, just by the bounce of it.

I watch for a bit, preparing myself, then run down the stairs to the front door, which I yank open and slam behind me. I slow myself before he can see me, and walk towards him at a shuffley pace, like it's a casual thing.

This is what you've been waiting for, isn't it? You want to know if this is Carl. I can see it now, the face you pull whenever I mention him. You get a greedy look in your eyes.

Sometimes I start saying things about him, then change the subject, just to annoy you.

Well . . .

the street

. . . it is him.

But I don't know that yet.

'That's a good ball,' I say.

He shrugs.

'Goes high.'

He shrugs again.

'Can you get it above the trees?'

He tilts his head back, thinks, then positions himself for a good throw and slams the ball down into the tarmac as hard as he can. It flies up, up up up, but not to the top of the trees. The trees are all the same height, right along the street, almost as high as the houses. They're silver birch, which is the only tree I can recognize apart from oak and fir. I could probably recognize an apple tree, but only if it had apples on it.

Mrs Sparks from next door, who's so old she's practically folded in half, once told me she could remember when the trees were so small they had to be held up with sticks. I don't really believe her. Mrs Sparks is the only one who's lived in the street right from when it was built. Mrs Sparks and the trees.

It's funny that she's called Sparks when she's almost dead.

The ball comes down really fast, and he catches it well, but with two hands. Before I came out he was catching with one, and he didn't have it perfect yet. He was on about 70 per cent, which isn't bad.

'Let's have a go.'

He looks me up and down slowly, then hands over the ball. It's warm and smooth, but also rough from where it's been hitting the road. It's a good size and a good weight. Feels just right in the hand. I steady myself. I have to do this well. If I throw like a spastic, he won't want to play with me.

It's not so easy to throw straight downwards. It isn't what you normally do. I think it through once, then – boof! – I go for it. It comes up so fast that if you angled it wrong it would hit you in the face and knock you out. Or kill you if it got you on a pressure point. Up it goes, as if it's jet-powered, then it seems to hover, floating, and suddenly you realize it's diving back at you.

For a second, I have a crazy thought – catch it in one hand! – but it comes down so fast, and I know from bitter experience that indecision is your worst enemy, so I cup both hands into a V and concentrate on not blinking. The ball flies in – thwack! – and tries its hardest to jump out again, but I lock my fingers together, holding the wriggling, squirming thing firm until it's calmed down.

In Australia, they catch balls upside-down to how we do. They have the little fingers on top and the thumbs underneath (see fig. 4). This has nothing to do with them living upside-down. You can catch a ball that way in the northern hemisphere, too, if you really want to, but you'll look a bit stupid.

I hand the ball back, like that was the easiest thing I ever did.

'Good ball,' I say.

'You can't break it. It's the only thing you can't break. You can't smash it or drown it or squash it or anything. It's the strongest thing in the world.'

'You could melt it,' I say. It just comes to me. Sometimes I think I must be really brainy.

27

FIGURE 4. HOW TO CATCH A BALL

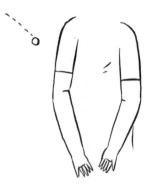

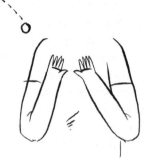

4A. ENGLISH STYLE   4B. AUSTRALIAN STYLE

His eyes flick up, and he looks at me properly for the first time, with the same expression Mum has when you say something she thinks you ought not to know. It's respect. I try not to smile.

'You reckon?' he says.

'Easy,' I say.

'How?'

'Matches.'

I think he's older than me. He's certainly bigger than me. But somehow I'm already in charge. It feels great. He's just looking at me now, waiting to see what I'll do next. It's the best feeling.

'I'll get some,' I say.

I almost tell him to wait there, then I realize it's even better if I don't say it. I walk back into the house, as slowly as I can make myself. Dad answers the door, but I'm in and past him before he can say anything, because I'm busy now and don't want to be interrupted.

Out back I scrabble through the cupboard where Mum keeps spare tins and loo rolls and cleaning products, and I soon find a box of matches – a big one with a sailing ship on the front.

I'm about to walk right out with it when I remember that Mum and Dad are having tea in the kitchen, which I have to go through. If I'm carrying a box of matches, there'll be questions. Only Dad's allowed to burn things, and even then not for fun. I can get from here to the hall without touching the floor – I've done it loads of times – but that won't help.* They'll still see me.

I stuff the matches up my sweatshirt, but I look pregnant. I push them round the back and tuck in, to hold the box in place, and decide to go for speed.

They stop me right off with that voice they can use.

'Ben!' It's Mum. She's figured something out. 'What are you doing?'

'There's a boy in the street.'

It sounds like someone's drowning kittens in the living room, which means Rachel and Lucy are watching pop videos. When they like someone, they scream. Girls are like that.

---

* I once knocked a plate off the wall when I was doing it, and I had to pretend I'd been throwing things around because it sounded too stupid to say I was practising crossing the room without touching the floor. The plates on the wall had only just gone up, too. They're not for eating off, they're for decoration. Donny says no one knows why, but when people hit forty they suddenly start wanting to put plates on walls. He says the urge lies dormant in the bloodstream until your fortieth birthday, then suddenly you wake up and think, 'That wall needs a plate on it.' I don't really understand what he's talking about. Dormant means sleepy.

'What's that up your jumper?' asks Mum.

She's got X-ray eyes. But for every extra power you get, you're also given a weakness. It's how things work. Hers is that she's a slow runner, and she hates getting up when she's in the middle of a cup of tea.

'He's waiting for me,' I say, and run for it.

She doesn't follow.

If you find out their weaknesses, you can win.

The boy holds the ball, and I hold the match. I still don't know his name, but it's not time to ask yet. I hold the match until my fingers burn, or near enough for me to act like it, anyway. The flame doesn't have much effect on the ball, other than making a bad smell and a small, black, ripply patch. It's a million miles from melting it. We try again, and it's still not much good.

Then he says he's got a better idea, and he opens the matchbox right up, takes out one match and puts the box down on the pavement. He's still holding the sleeve. He puts the ball into the box, on top of all the matches. He looks up at me with a glint in his eye. He's grinning, and so am I. When you're excited, sometimes it feels like you need a wee, even though you don't.

He lights the match that he's holding and drops it into the box, right on top of the first row's purple lighting bits. There's a massive crackle and fizz, and the whole thing goes up, and half a second later there's another big one as the second row catches alight. The flames are as high as my knee, and they're so bright the ball completely disappears inside the fire. You can smell it, though, giving off a really nasty pong, but in a good way because we know we did it.

The fire doesn't last long. There's a black, lumpy mess left behind which smokes and steams like an asteroid that's only just landed. We kneel down and blow on it to make the ball cool enough to pick up. I want to be the first to reach in, but he beats me to it. The ball's not ready, though, and he drops it straight away, with a yelp. The ball's really wonked. It bounces in a zigzag now, back and forward like it's gone nuts. We both laugh at how it's bouncing, and when it stops in the gutter I go and crouch over it.

The surface of the whole ball is blistered and bobbly like the worst zitty face you've ever seen – as bad as Alison from the end of the street whose cheeks look like sick. It's gone black all over, too, and it's not round any more, but a saggy oval.

It's not a puddle of rubber, though. I mean, you can't say we've actually melted it. But we've certainly bust it, which was the point. We've definitely won, even though it seems like a shame now because it was a good ball, and now it isn't.

We chuck it around for a bit, which is a laugh because you don't know where it's going to bounce, but it's annoying, too, and after a while I'm only pretending to enjoy it. I can tell he's a bit bored as well. We need something new.

'My Dad's got a chainsaw,' I say. 'He's been using it all afternoon, but now he's having a tea break. D'you want to see it?'

He shrugs, but I can tell by the look on his face that he's keen.

I take him round the side, where you have to go over the gate. I climb it first. I don't go for a record time or anything, I just make sure I do it right. I can open it from the inside, then, but he tells me to shut it because he wants to go over the top, too. I don't tell him about the loose bit of fence, and he slips a little, but he gets over well enough.

31

All the houses in the street are the same, apart from the flats that became a mental home, and they all have a garden gate round the side. Mrs Sparks leaves hers unlocked for me, so I can get my balls when they go over without having to ring her bell. Her grass is so long that tennis balls are a nightmare. Mum says I should mow it for her, but it'd feel funny offering.

You'd think the houses were massive, but they're not because each house is actually two houses. They're cut in half. If you count the front doors, it's obvious. Mrs Sparks has got the other half of ours, and you can hear her telly coming through the wall. She turns it up loudest for *Highway*.

Me and the boy are now in the garden, surrounded by the sawn-up branch, looking down at the chainsaw, and suddenly I'm wondering whether this was such a good idea. I'm not supposed to touch it, and when I mentioned the chainsaw I thought we'd just come and have a look, but now we're looking at it, it seems like we can't just walk away or I'll seem like a total girl.

I'm hoping Dad'll come out and tell us off, but I look up at the house and the curtains are all closed. It's the time of day when it's not dark yet, but if you're inside you have to put the lights on anyway. Curtains are a big thing for Mum. Opening and closing them. You never know when she's going to suddenly jump up and rush all over the house doing it. She tries to get help, but no one else shares the passion.

'Is it heavy?' he asks.

'Yeah,' I say. 'Hurts your arms if you're not used to it.'

He leans over and tests the chainsaw's weight. Then suddenly he's standing there, holding it at his waist like it's a machine gun. If Dad comes out now, we'll be in big trouble.

'How do you start it?' he asks.

'There's a string on a handle at the back. You have to yank it.'

He touches the string, but it almost makes him drop the saw, so he moves his hand back to where it was.

'It's too heavy. You'll have to do it.'

My eyes flick up to the house. Still nothing's moving in there. I can hear Rachel and Lucy, who are either sticking pins into each other or still watching videos. I could have said I didn't know how to start it. That would have been a better thing to say. But it's too late now.

'I'm not supposed to,' I say, quietly.

'Says who? SAYS WHO?'

It's like he's angry. I don't know why. His face is suddenly twisted and nasty. If he'd looked like this when I went out to say hello, I would have gone straight back inside. He's not big, but he's scary. He's got that thing in his voice which makes you think everything will get worse if you don't do what he says.

'My Dad,' I say.

'And you're scared of him, are you?'

He beams his eyes at me, and I notice for the first time that they're bright blue – the colour of empty swimming pools – so blue you don't want to look straight into them. His skin's pale and his hair's a dark, short crop that makes the blue seem even bluer. It doesn't look right. It's like his face is in black and white, but his eyes are in colour.

'No,' I say.

'Well, then.'

I don't move.

'Come on,' he says. 'It'll be fun.'

This has gone all wrong. I'm really not in charge now.

I step towards him and put my fingers into the handle that starts the chainsaw. I can't think of any way out of it.

'I'm not supposed to.' It sounds like I'm begging him.

'Come on! Don't be a girl!'

I've got the starter in my hand, but I can't make myself pull it.

'COME ON!' he shouts. 'What are you waiting for, you baby?'

I give the string a yank, just like I've seen Dad do, but the engine only splutters. Second time the same thing happens.

'What's wrong with you?' he's saying. 'Why are you such a weed? Can't you even do it?'

I pull with everything I've got, and suddenly the saw comes alive in his hands, roaring like a motorbike.

'Hoooo-hooooooooooooooo!' he crows, waving it around in a big circle. It's so heavy and noisy that it looks like the saw is moving him, not the other way round. You can hardly see the teeth of it now, they're whirring so fast.

I step back, but not so far he'll think I'm scared.

He tests it out on a small branch first, and it goes through like there's nothing there. Then he slashes at a thick log on the ground, and the saw growls and jerks in his hands, as if it could fly off in any direction. Chips of wood spray everywhere.

I take a couple more steps back and bump against Dad, who's run out into the garden, but you couldn't hear him over the sound of the saw, which is so loud it's like everything else has become a silent movie.

Dad says something to me, but without a caption there's no way of knowing what it is.

'Switch that off!' he shouts.

The boy doesn't hear him. I wish I'd asked his name now, in case anything bad happens. I can see that Dad doesn't want to get any closer because, if the boy turns round, he'll get him with the saw.

When there's a pause in the cutting, Dad shouts again.

'OI! YOU! SWITCH THAT OFF RIGHT NOW!'

This time he hears. He turns to face my dad, and stares at him. Dad stares back. Neither of them moves. The teeth of the saw are still whizzing round, cutting the air between them.

'I said, turn that off,' says Dad. It's less noisy now the boy isn't sawing.

The boy still just stares at him. He doesn't speak.

'NOW!'

The boy changes the angle of the saw, and props it against his hip. In this position, he's not just holding it, he's pointing it at Dad.

Dad's face goes white. It's not like a chainsaw is something you can grab off someone. There's no socket you can switch off, either. In front of this kid, for all his size, Dad's helpless.

'Who are you?' says Dad.

There's no answer, so Dad turns, grabs me by the elbow and shouts, 'DID YOU BRING HIM HERE?'

I nod, and windmill my arm so he has to let go. My eyes are stinging now. I glance up at the house, and I can see Rachel and Lucy through the patio doors. They're standing between the curtains and the window, looking out at us. Mum is up by the back door. I run over to her, and she puts an arm round me. I'm not even embarrassed.

Dad takes a step towards the boy. Then one more. The saw is still going. If Dad reached his hand out now, it would be cut to bits.

'What's your name?' asks Dad.

The boy doesn't answer. It's like he's in a trance. You can't tell if he's threatening to attack Dad, or if he's just gone into a daydream.

'Put it down. Put it down, now.' Dad's trying to sound calm, but you can tell it's an effort.

Still the boy just stands there, his body braced against the weight and speed of the saw, staring towards Dad, looking at him or through him, I can't tell which.

'What's your name?' Dad asks again.

After a long gap, the boy says, 'I've just moved in.'

'Where?'

The boy waves the saw around, as if he's practising his slicing technique, as if he's forgotten Dad's there.

'Where?' says Dad.

He doesn't answer. He just slices the air, calm as anything.

'Put it down. Put the saw down before you hurt yourself.'

The boy looks at him. Even though he only comes up to Dad's shoulder, it's like the boy's looking down and Dad's looking up. For a moment, the boy seems to be smiling.

'Say "please",' he says.

Dad rubs his face and thinks.

'Say "please",' repeats the boy, in the voice you'd use to a baby.

'Please,' says Dad, eventually.

The boy tosses the saw on to the grass, as if he's suddenly bored of it. It lands with a thunk and goes quiet. Before the saw has even hit the ground, the boy sets off past Dad and past me and out into the street. I can hear him laughing as he goes off.

If it wasn't for Olly, that would have been an end of it between me and Carl. I'm not an idiot. But you can't always choose your friends, can you?

Or maybe you don't know that because you probably haven't got any.

the park

Me and Olly are at the racetrack. It's not really a racetrack. It's a fenced-off bit of the park which has been concreted over, but in the middle there's a figure eight of concrete in a different colour. We reckon it was probably supposed to be a racetrack, but they never finished it – or maybe it used to be a racetrack, but they dismantled it. Either way, it doesn't make any difference to us. It still works. We often bike round and round it while we're talking, or we do skids on the gravel in the middle, and every so often we actually race. We sometimes start from opposite ends, so when you get to the crossroads in the middle there's nearly a crash each time and you have to see who bottles out first. It's always Olly.

He's a ginga. That's ginga to rhyme with singer. He hates it when you call him that. You can also call him ginge, which he hates just as much. The sad thing is, there's no polite word for it. He's more orange than you'd ever think was possible. You don't normally see hair Olly's colour. In fact, you don't normally see anything that colour. The only other place I've ever seen it is on Donny's 'DANGER: HAZARDOUS WASTE' sticker.

Because he's my best friend, I take the piss out of Olly for everything except the hair. He's the only person in the world who's looking forward to going bald.

Me and Olly are at the track. We're not doing much in particular, sort of trying to see how long we can stay in one place without putting a foot down, but we're not doing it properly. We're not watching each other or timing it or anything.

It's Olly who notices him first. He's at the other side of the track. He's doing the same thing we're doing, except he's really good at it. He can stay there for ages without going forwards or putting a foot down or even wobbling. He's not looking at us, he's just doing it. He's pretending he hasn't seen us, but you can tell he's noticed he's being watched because he starts concentrating even harder on his balancing.

'Shit!' I say. I don't know why, I just say it.

Even though it's ages since I last saw him, he's still wearing the same red tracksuit. It's supposed to be Arsenal, but it's not the real thing. If it was mine, I'd put a '7' on the back for Liam Brady, and get Olly to wear a '10', which is Frank Stapleton.

'What?' says Olly. 'D'you know him?'

'Yeah.'

'What's his name?'

'Don't know.'

'Who is he?'

'Moved into my street. He's a nutter.'

Then suddenly Olly's cycling over to him, which is the last thing I was going to do. Olly's like that. He's always curious. Maybe I shouldn't have said 'nutter' because I didn't mean it in a good way, I meant it in a bad way, but if you don't explain it properly, it can sound like a compliment.

I can't just stay there on my own, while Olly goes over, so I spin my pedals into place and follow him. My gears crunch as I go over, changing down from what I was using for balancing. You're not supposed to start off in a high gear, it's bad for them.

'Hi,' says Olly.

The boy doesn't answer. He just looks at Olly and gives a little upwards nod.

'That's a good bike,' says Olly.

The boy shrugs and looks away, into the distance.

If Olly had any sense, he'd play it cool, but he doesn't know how. 'What's your name?' he asks.

The boy slowly turns his head towards Olly, and checks us both out, one by one. I can't tell if he even recognizes me.

'Carl,' he says. 'I'm Carl.'

'Olly,' says Olly. 'And he's Ben.'

Carl nods again, this time at me. It's exactly the same nod he gave to Olly, as if I'm a complete stranger.

'Let's go for a ride,' he says.

Then suddenly he's off. Not just fast, but superfast. It's a challenge. Normally you wouldn't just follow someone like that, but he does it so quickly that we know, if we don't go for it straight away, we'll be left so far behind we'll never catch up. We've got only a split second to decide.

Me and Olly look at each other. My instinct is to go, but something tells me not to. Then Olly's off, and I'm after him.

Carl's miles ahead, and he doesn't even look round to see if we're following. He goes down the main path, past the bowling green, towards the gates, but just before the park exit he veers left, and we follow, juddering our bikes over the grass. Past the tennis courts we get back on the path, and Carl loops left up to the football pitches, then he skids a U-ey and comes right towards us doing a kamikaze face-off. Neither of us is prepared for it, so we don't get out of the way, but at the last second he veers off to the right and disappears. There's a slope there. It's the steepest slope in the whole park. No one's ever cycled down it.

Me and Olly have stopped now. We've both got our heads cocked on one side, listening. There's nothing, then a loud whoop – a jiggled one because of the bumps in the grass – as he does the slope. We can hear when he hits the path because his whoop goes smooth.

There's no crash. He's done it.

We cycle over to the edge, and he's at the bottom, looking up at us.

'Come on,' he says. Then he cycles off.

We've spent whole days up here, deciding whether or not to do it, but we never have. Then suddenly Olly's up, over the edge, and down, whooping all the way as loud as he can. He doesn't even stop at the bottom, but goes straight after Carl.

'It's easy,' he shouts up to me, over his shoulder.

'I know,' I shout back.

My chest has gone tight, and my throat feels as if I'm in the middle of swallowing something, even though I'm not. Olly's now got as far as the tennis courts. He's cycling on, but he keeps flicking his head back to look at me. I have to go for it.

Gripping the handlebars as tight as I can, I launch myself off.

I can't get out a good whoop until I'm halfway down. My whole body's being shaken up like I'm in an air crash, and my tummy's still somewhere at the top of the hill because I accelerated too fast for it, but it's a great feeling, and I haven't even got to the bottom before I start wanting to do the whole thing again, but there's no time now. I have to catch up.

I find Olly at the park gates, one foot on the ground, the other on a pedal, his bike resting between his legs at an angle. He's looking all around, squinting.

'Lost him,' he says.

I do a 360 of the park. No sign. He's not on the main path

back to the racetrack, he's not on the road down to the shops and, even though it's out of sight, we know he can't be on the path round the tennis courts or we would have run into him. That leaves only the alley. You wouldn't normally go up there on a bike, since it just goes to the bridge, which has steps the height of more than a house. It's for getting over the railway tracks, but only on foot because it's too small for cars and too high for bikes. There's nowhere else he can be, though.

We head down the alley, not speaking. We're both a bit excited. I don't know why.

At the end of the alley, you turn left, and the stairs go straight up ahead of you. When we get to the corner, there he is, miles above us, at the top of the steps, with his bike leaning against the wall next to him. He's just standing there, looking down.

'What've you been doing?' he says. 'Knitting?'

'No,' I say. It's not a brilliant answer, but I can't think of anything better.

'I've been here hours,' he says.

Then he takes something out of his pocket and chucks it down at us. It hits the wall right by my head and bounces off my bike wheel. It's an acorn. I can't reach it without getting off my bike. I can't just leave it there, though. So I get off, shove my racer against the wall, pick up the acorn, and chuck it back at him, but it's pointless. I can't even get it halfway up the stairs. Gravity makes it impossible (see fig. 5).

Then he's got a whole fistful of them, and they're coming down at us like bullets. Olly's trying to chuck them back, too, but they're not getting anywhere near. The only thing to do is to rush him.

I pick up my bike and put the crossbar on my shoulder. The front wheel gives me a bit of an acorn shield. 'Chaaaaaaaaaaaa

FIGURE 5.
ACORN ATTACK SCENARIO

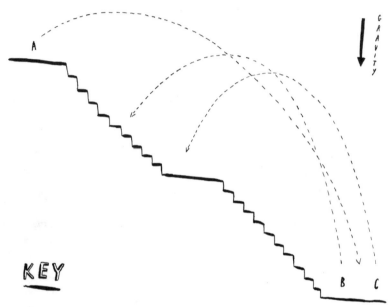

A

GRAVITY

KEY

A) CARL

B) ME

C) OLLY

------ FLIGHT OF ACORN

〰 STAIRS

aaaaarrrrrrrrrrrrggggggggge!' I shout, and run up the stairs as fast as I can.

Olly does the same, right behind. The acorns are really pelting us now, then suddenly they stop. I look up. Carl's gone.

At the top, we remount, and zoom right across the bridge, which only takes about five seconds. You can't see down to the railway tracks because they built the walls too high to see over, which I think is evil. Normally you'd stop and bounce in the middle because, if two of you jump up and down at once, you can make the bridge jiggle, but there's no time for that now.

When we get to the far end, Carl's on his bike, halfway down the steps, his head turned so he's looking up at us. If we had some acorns now we could really get him, but we threw them all back instead of keeping some as ammo.

'Watch this,' he says.

Then he lets go of the brake, and he's cycling down the stairs. Starting from halfway up. This is totally mental! There's nothing at the bottom except concrete. Olly and me have never even *thought* of cycling down the bridge stairs. You'd have to be nuts to even have the idea. Now Carl's doing it right in front of our eyes.

His bike's rocking up and down like it's having a fit and, as he gets nearer the bottom, the bike goes faster and faster, the weight of it going backwards and forwards in a way that looks all wrong, and then, when he's only a few steps from the bottom, his front wheel goes sideways on the step, and the back wheel flies up, and Carl's thrown into the air, over the handlebars and splat on his face with the bike clattering down on top of him.

It ought to be funny, but it isn't. Carl lies there, not moving, and no one laughs.

Me and Olly leave our bikes at the top and run down as fast as we can. By the time we get to the bottom, Carl has stood up. He's staring at his palms, which are grazed and black. You can see little bits of gravel nestling in bloody slits in his hands. Just above his ear, there's a patch of hair that's gone red and spongy.

'There was a stone on the step. I hit a stone.'

Me and Olly just nod.

'Are you OK?' I ask.

'*Yes.*' He says it angrily, like I'm being nosy.

We stare at him while he brushes at his hands and dabs at the mark on his head with a finger. I pick up his bike and check the wheels for him. They both spin OK. The front one gives a slight squeak, but there doesn't seem to be any real damage. He takes his bike off me and checks the wheels for himself.

He fiddles with the bike for ages, and we just watch.

'What d'you leave your bikes up there for?' he says, as if we're the ones that have done something wrong, not him. The way he says it, you can almost believe him.

Without answering, me and Olly go back up the stairs to get them. On the way up, there's silence except for the sound of our feet on the steps. Even when we're too high up for Carl to hear if we're saying anything, we still don't speak.

We carry our bikes slowly back down. Carl's already on his by the time we get to the bottom.

'Come on,' he says, and cycles off. I don't think either of us really wants to follow now, but we can't not. It's strange that he doesn't want to go home, but neither of us says anything.

Carl leads us down Francis Road and round the back of the council houses where I've never been before, under the railway bridge, in and out of the dump, slaloming round the huge skips, and through the park a couple more times. He doesn't do any more stunts, but it's still a chase, and the whole thing's a laugh. Even though he's just moved here, he knows places I've never been before. Or maybe it's just that he goes anywhere he fancies and assumes no one's going to stop him. It's good fun. Not as good as before he crashed, but still good.

At dinner time we end up outside Olly's. Normally I'd go in with him, but because Carl's there I don't. As we're saying bye, Carl asks us if we'll be in the same place tomorrow.

Me and Olly look at each other, then Olly says yes, even though that wasn't the look I gave him.

I ride home with Carl, stopping at his first, then I go on to mine. Inside, Mum asks me who I was with, and I just say Olly.

the pilgrimage

It's not long after breakfast when I go over to Olly's. His mum answers the door. She's where Olly gets the ginga genes from. Genes is the name for the bits of you that you get from your parents, which scientists say is almost everything, so when your parents are telling you off you can blame it on your genes and make it their fault.

On Olly's mum, the hair looks nice. It's different with women. When Dad talks to her, he goes red and sweaty like when he's trying to fit a plug or programme the video.

'He's not here,' she says.

Olly's mum never says hello or goodbye, but sometimes she does turn up with a plate of biscuits. His dad's a bit scary and never talks. When he answers the door, which is hardly ever, he always looks annoyed that it's me, but he looks annoyed most of the time anyway, so it's probably not my fault.

'Where's he gone?'

'Don't know. Went off with a boy I've never seen before. Called for him on his bike.'

Suddenly my heart's pounding so hard I can hear it in my ears. It's like she's just hit me in the face. I turn round to head for the park, but it's hard to get Olly's gate open when you're on a bike. As I'm struggling to get through, Olly's mum says, 'Bye, then.'

She's smiling, as if there's something funny I don't understand. She's like that. It's typical that the only time she'll say bye is when she doesn't mean it.

'Bye,' I say, trying to sound normal, but she's already shut the door behind her.

I peg it, fast as a race, ignoring the burn in my legs which comes on before I'm even halfway there, but as soon as I get to the park I find myself jamming on the brakes. I can see them in the distance. They're at the track, on their bikes, in the corner spot that me and Olly always use, where you can sit with both feet on the pedals, holding yourself upright with the fence posts. To look at them, you'd think they'd known each other for years.

Part of me just wants to turn round and go straight back home.

I could do that. Wait for Olly to come after me. Show him that what he's done is wrong. But I can't just leave them there. I couldn't spend the whole day on my own, knowing they're together, doing stuff without me. I have to go over, even though it makes me feel sick to think of riding up to them, interrupting their conversation and saying hi as if I'm the newcomer.

I cycle towards them and swerve on to the track without slowing down. I aim for Olly and ride right at him, with my legs pumping as hard as they can. I'm really zooming, completely ignoring the figure eight, just heading straight for him as if I'm going to smash into his legs at top speed, then at the last second I give a dab on the front brake and a huge squeeze on the back one. I lean away, plant a foot and skid right up to him, timing it perfectly so he can't help flinching because it seems there's no way I'll stop in time, but I do, almost on top of him, our tyres brushing together like a tiny kiss at the final second. A pro couldn't have timed it better.

After that, I don't feel I have to say hi. I glance at Carl to see if he's impressed.

Doesn't look like he is.

'Idiot,' says Olly. 'Nearly broke my legs.'

'Didn't, though, did I?'

Olly just tuts.

There's a silence. I don't have anything to say, and neither does Olly by the look of it. I want to know what they were talking about, but I can't just ask.

Eventually, Carl says, 'We're going on a trip.'

'When?' I ask.

'Now,' he says. 'To Wembley.'

'Wembley?'

'Yeah. Wembley Stadium.'

Wembley's miles away. Literally. In a car it would take ages. On a bike it's barely even possible. It's ten times further than Olly and me have ever gone.

'It's a thingummy,' says Olly. 'When you go to see something because it's famous. There's a word for it.'

'We can't get to Wembley,' I say. 'It's miles.'

'Miles isn't a problem,' says Carl. 'We can go miles. Bikes are made to go miles.'

'But ... but ...' I want to say that it's impossible, that it's too far, that it's just not allowed, but I can't think of a way to put it that won't sound bad. 'How are we going to find it?' I say.

Carl turns and points. Far away, near the horizon, above the tennis courts, are Wembley's twin towers, like two big meringues.

'Just because we can see them from here doesn't mean we can find them,' I say.

'Why not?'

'Because we don't know the way.'

'Yes, we do. It's that way.'

'That's not a way. It's a direction.'

'Same thing.'

'We don't know which are the right roads.'

'If it's the right direction, it's the right roads.'

'But you can't always see it. When we can't see it, we won't know which direction it is.'

'It isn't going to move, is it. It doesn't run away when you're not looking at it.'

'But you can hardly ever see it. There's too many houses.'

'That's part of the fun, isn't it.' says Carl. 'We head in that direction and see if we get there.'

'What if we get lost?'

Carl shrugs.

I look at Olly. His face is serious, but I can't tell if he's scared.

'It's too far,' I say.

'Olly says it's about half an hour in a car, so if a car goes at thirty, that means it's fifteen miles. It's easy.'

'That'll take all day. What about lunch?'

Carl pulls something small and crumpled from his pocket and snaps it open in front of me, pulling it taut with two hands. It's a ten-pound note.

'Where d'you get that?'

'Same place I get everything,' he says.

I hate it when people do that. Give you an answer that isn't an answer, just to make you ask more questions so you sound desperate. I don't want to play that game, so I just stare at him. That's when I notice something weird. The spot above his ear where he banged his head is still caked with blood. The hair's in clumps, like tiny, red icicles. My eyes flick down to his hands. I can see his right palm, which is resting on his thigh, and it's

49

also just the same as yesterday. The graze is still black and red. It hasn't been washed, and there's no plaster.

Carl sees where I'm looking and flips his hand over.

Olly's gazing dreamily at the twin towers. 'There's a word for it,' he says. 'P something.'

Sometimes Olly's too dumb to know when he ought to be scared. When I've done risky things with Olly in the past, he only gets scared the day after. He goes to casualty more often than most people go to the dentist.

'You don't have to come,' says Carl. 'If you're too chicken, we'll do it without you.'

I want to ask Olly if he really thinks it's allowed, but I can't in front of Carl.

'Pilgrimage,' I say. 'It's a pilgrimage.'

'Doesn't sound right,' says Olly.

It's not just talk. They're going to do it. And I can't let them go without me. I can't just sit at home and let Carl take Olly off like that. I don't have any choice except to join in. If you think I do – if you think I should have turned round and gone home – it just shows how stupid you are, and how you don't understand anything about anyone.

If you go along but act scared, you're no better off than if you chicken out altogether. Since I'm going to do it, I might as well look confident. I might as well act like it could have been my idea.

'Come on,' I say. 'What are we waiting for?'

And I set off. Just like that. They have to follow me.

I don't want it to look like I'm trying too hard, but I set up a fast pace. Before we're even out of the park, Carl overtakes me. I can hear his front wheel squeak as he goes past.

*

Kenton Road's two lanes in each direction, really fast, always full. It's so obvious I'm not allowed to cycle there that no one's ever bothered to say it. Carl doesn't even hesitate. He steers straight into the flow of traffic, as if he was a car. Me and Olly don't have a moment to think about it. We just follow.

The buses and lorries go by so close that each one makes you wobble, the air around them shoving you towards the kerb, then sucking you back again after they pass. None of the drains is at the same height as the road, and when you see one coming you have about a second to decide if you're going to swing out between the cars or just ride over the dip and hope it doesn't knock you off. It's scary, but not in a fun way.

Carl turns round, and grins. You can tell he's loving it. He shouts something I don't hear and points across the road to where we last saw the towers, then swings out into the traffic, steering himself right across to the fast lane. Without thinking, I follow him, and so does Olly behind me. A big truck hoots and flashes at us, brakes squealing, but we make it. Right in the middle of the road, Carl stops, and we pull in behind him.

'That way,' he says.

The traffic is now whizzing by on both sides of us. We're doing a right turn in the way you'd do it in a car, not going up to the lights and crossing there, but stopping in the middle and letting everyone go round us while we wait for a gap in the oncoming traffic. Because we're only on bikes, no one stops behind us, so we've got two lanes on each side, zooming past, with lots of cars hooting and swerving at the last minute. It's a bit like being a skittle.

We wait for ages, but there are no gaps. None of us speaks. We've all got our feet in position, one on the ground, one on a raised pedal, and our heads are angled in the same direction, looking ahead of us at the endless stream of cars, waiting for our moment. There are lots of half-moments, when I think it might just be possible, but I stop myself at the last second, and judge the gaps as they go past to figure out if I would have made it or not.

It's during one of these half-chances that Carl goes for it. The fast lane's empty, but there's a Volvo tanking along in the slow lane that looks much too close, and as soon as Carl sets off it's clear there's no turning back, and also that he's in the wrong gear because he's got no acceleration, and it's like the whole thing's in slow motion, it's like the whole thing's been timed exactly so he'll go smack into the front bumper of the Volvo because, even though it hasn't happened yet, it's so close and so unavoidable that Carl might as well be dead already. I can see exactly where the crash is going to happen, with Carl right in the middle of the lane at the second the car gets there. Carl's not stopping, and the Volvo's going much too fast to stop, but it hits the brakes anyway and skids, hurtling forwards with its tyres locked, screaming against the tarmac. It seems like Carl's got about half a second to live, but suddenly the shrieking stops, the wheels turn and the car swerves out into the fast lane, the whole body of it tilting, the driver's eyes almost popping out as he goes past right in front of us, squeezing through the gap between Carl's back wheel and my front wheel, and then it's all over, and Carl's standing there on the opposite side of the road, in one piece, grinning.

There's a smell in the air of burnt rubber, same as when we tried to melt Carl's ball.

He gets off his bike and does a victory dance, waving his arms in the air and wiggling his bum. It barely seems possible that he's there, still alive, dancing, and all I can do is stare, everything vanishing from my mind except the sight of Carl, in his red tracksuit, wiggling his bum on the other side of the street. He touches the tip of a finger to his tongue and draws a 'I' on an imaginary blackboard in the air, then he makes a circle with his finger and thumb, and shakes it in our direction. With the cars thumping past between us, it's like he's in a different world. It's as if I'm looking through a screen at him, as if he's on TV and I'm real.

I know there's nothing more dangerous than someone who's fearless, and I know I ought to be scared of him, but I don't really feel it. What I feel, more than anything, is excited. It's strange, because I don't like him, and I know he's bad, but I want to be with him. I want to be on the other side of the street, dancing, looking back at Olly.

Then Olly goes past me. I look up the road and there's a long gap, so I cross, too. Even if it had only been a short gap, I would have gone for it.

'Did you see his face?' I say. 'In the Volvo?'

I pull it, puffing my cheeks out as far as they'll go and pushing my eyebrows down towards my nose.

Olly and Carl laugh, and we all pull the face, seeing who can do it best, then we're off again. It's just an ordinary road now, with houses on each side and only a few cars. After Kenton Road, it's the easiest thing in the world. We slalom all over the place, sometimes turning round and pulling the Volvo face to the person behind to try and make them laugh. We're all excited like we've just won something, and everything makes us crack up, even stupid little things like bumping into each other. It's probably because we nearly got killed.

The road we're on looks just like the one where I live, but the slope of it's different. You always know which road is yours. After a bit, we get to a crossroads. There's a line on the tarmac showing that we're the ones who have to stop. I think I've been here in a car, but I don't really know where we are. It's not anywhere I've been on a bike. All I know is that home's behind us.

There's been no sight of Wembley since the park.

'That way,' says Carl, pointing straight across the junction. He doesn't slow down for the white line or wait to see if we agree about the direction, he just goes, and we follow.

The roads wiggle and turn, and for ages there's not even a glimpse of the stadium. Half the time we're on quiet streets with houses and half the time we're on big roads with shops, but after Kenton Road nothing seems scary any more. It's like we're invincible.

When we get to a roundabout – the biggest one I've ever done on a bike, with cars coming at us from every angle like a video game – we just have to guess which exit to take, and even Carl admits he's not really sure.

Then we see a railway and follow it in what feels like the right direction. The tracks lead us to Preston Road station, which means we're going the right way because Preston Road is the Tube stop between us and Wembley. Just after that, we see the towers again, and it feels like a miracle because they really are closer. Not just closer, but bigger.

The idea that you really can go anywhere – that you don't have to ask anyone, and that nothing bad is going to happen – is like suddenly discovering the best game in the world. Just because somewhere's far away, that doesn't mean it's more dangerous. It doesn't make sense that your little bit is the only safe bit. Somewhere far away is somewhere near for the people who live there, and where I live would be far away to them. There are people everywhere, which means everywhere's near for someone, which means there's probably nothing wrong with it.

It's obvious, once you think about it, but today it's a new and completely amazing thought.

I haven't looked at my watch once, and I'm hardly even tired at the moment we go round a corner and see the long, straight path that goes from where we are right to the bottom of the twin towers. We've seen it on telly. Everyone in the world's probably seen it on telly, on Cup Final day, with thousands of football fans bobbing towards the stadium, like the whole place is carpeted with people. And now we're there. Just us. We've got it all to ourselves.

Olly's the first one to whoop, but as soon as he starts Carl and me both join in and hold it as loud and as long as we can while we peg it down the path, our hearts pounding, riding faster and faster towards the stadium steps, racing but not racing, just all of us going as quick as we can, together, celebrating that we've done it, that we've got there, to Wembley. It's the best feeling in the world.

We muck around at the stadium for ages, riding up and down all the ramps and skidding in the puddles (which are huge). The car park in front is so massive that you can't look at it without wanting to ride in long swoops all around. There's no one there except us, us and the pigeons, who flap away in clouds however fast you ride up to them. It's Carl's idea to try and run them over, but none of us even gets close.

We're so busy that we don't once think of having lunch. We just find that we're on the way home, without anyone having to say it's time to go, and even though it's the longest distance I've ever cycled, the whole trip is somehow imprinted on the brain, and it's really easy to get back. At each junction, you just remember it and know which way to turn. We don't even have to talk about it. We all just go the same way.

I've always wondered how grown-ups know how to get everywhere, and now I understand. There's no magic to it. Or if there is, it's magic we can all do.

As we're riding back, I remember that I still haven't told Olly what I know about Carl. I haven't told him what Carl did with the chainsaw – how he lost it and behaved like a freak.

I'd been thinking that I couldn't wait to tell – to put him off Carl and get things back to normal – but now I'm wondering if I should keep it to myself for a while. Maybe having three of us is more fun than two. Maybe I should just stay quiet and see if Carl turns out to be OK. With him around, things happen. New things.

We get to Olly's house first. It's almost dark. As we're saying bye, Carl asks Olly what his number is. Olly goes into the house and comes out with it written on a bit of paper.

'I put Ben's down as well,' he says as he hands it over.

'Can't he do it himself ?'

Because he's saying it to Olly instead of me, I can't give an answer, but it makes me feel weird that he's said it – that when we've all had fun he should suddenly act like he wants an argument.

'What's yours?' asks Olly. You can tell he's changing the subject on purpose.

Carl doesn't say anything, but takes the pen, yanks Olly's sleeve up and writes in huge numbers on his forearm, making him laugh and squirm as he does it.

'D'you want it?' he says to me, after he's finished.

I shrug a yes. Carl takes my arm and writes on the back of

my hand in tiny, smudged digits. I pretend I haven't noticed the difference, or don't care, secretly straining to come up with a joke that would get him back – that would balance things out again – but I can't think of anything.

We're in the same spot as where Olly's mum told me the two of them had gone to the park without me. It feels like ages ago, but it was only this morning. Now, with Carl gripping my wrist and scratching minuscule numbers hard into my skin, I get the same feelings all over again: that I'm being left out; that Carl's ranked me below Olly.

Olly doesn't look at me as he says bye.

In the bath, later, I wash and wash it till it hurts, till there's no trace.

olly's house

It's a regular thing with me and Olly that on Saturdays, while we're waiting for *Final Score*, we put on the wrestling and copy the moves on the living-room floor.

When Carl joins in, it becomes a different game. The fighting is more like proper fighting, especially when it's me v Carl. He can beat us both, but with Olly he's gentle. He deliberately gets the two of them twisted up into funny positions, and they're always laughing. With me, he just grabs hold of an arm or wrist or ear, and twists as hard as he can until I submit, then he makes me say it again and again before he actually stops.

He never hurts Olly like that. Just me. Olly knows it, too, but he doesn't care.

Olly actually likes him. That's the problem. He likes being in a group, instead of a pair. So from Wembley right till the end of the holidays, the three of us are a unit. It's never just me and Olly any more. It's always all of us.

That's not how I want it but, if Olly phones him, I can't turn Carl away. And I can't stay away myself, or I'd have nothing to do. You have to act together to keep someone out. When you're friends with someone you do it all the time, without thinking. Just the way you are together makes it obvious no one else is invited. But with Carl, Olly doesn't do it. He opens the doors and lets him right in, without even asking me.

It's always Olly's house now. We never get invited to Carl's and don't go to mine either. Dad would go mental. I'd never be able to explain how Carl's become my friend. I haven't had any say in it, but Dad wouldn't understand that.

As soon as I get a good moment, alone with Olly, I tell him the chainsaw story, but it's too late. By then, Olly knows I don't get on with Carl, and the way it comes out the story doesn't sound believable. It just sounds like I've made something up to put Olly off him.

Olly doesn't tell me I'm lying, he just says, 'So?'

So I tell the story again, more vividly, with more details of how mad Carl seemed. And still Olly just says, 'So?'

You can't argue against that. It doesn't give you anything to work with.

Sometimes I think maybe Olly doesn't really like Carl, either. He just likes the way Carl treats him, compared to how Carl treats me. Before, when it was only two of us, I was definitely in charge. Now everything's upside-down, and it's Carl in charge, with me at the bottom of the heap. It's always me that gets hurt, or teased, or left behind, never Olly, and definitely never Carl.

If Olly thought I always bossed him around too much, he should have said something. To just let someone new take over is stupid because Carl makes everything worse. It's obvious. But Olly's always been like that. He wants everything the same for ages and ages, then suddenly he'll decide he likes something new, and that's it. There's never a warning, and he never changes his mind. Nothing I can say about Carl would make any difference.

Olly will usually do what other people want, but he'll always think what he wants. On little things, you can persuade him;

FIGURE 6. GAMES SPOILT BY CARL

GAME	HOW CARL RUINS IT
MONOPOLY	GETTING BORED WHEN HE STARTS LOSING, FLICKING HOUSES AROUND, AND MAKING YOU EMBARRASSED TO CARE ABOUT PRETEND MONEY
CLUEDO	LOOKING AT WHO DID IT BEFORE IT'S TIME
SNOOKER	HITTING BALLS OFF THE TABLE WHEN HE STARTS LOSING AND COMPLAINING THAT ONLY BABIES PLAY ON A TABLE AS SMALL AS OLLY'S
TABLE TENNIS	HITTING THE BALL STRAIGHT AT YOUR HEAD WHEN HE STARTS LOSING
DARTS	AIMING AT THINGS IN THE GARAGE THAT AREN'T THE BOARD
FOOTBALL	FOULING, AND NOT GETTING THE BALL WHEN HE'S THE ONE THAT'S KICKED IT OVER THE FENCE
CRICKET	NOT ADMITTING HE'S OUT WHEN HE OBVIOUSLY IS
CYCLING	TURNING IT INTO DARE ON THE RAILWAY TRACKS, AND CALLING YOU A CHICKEN IF YOU WON'T RUN RIGHT ACROSS
WRESTLING	HURTING ME
COMPUTER GAMES	DOESN'T. EVEN CARL CAN'T TELL A COMPUTER WHAT TO DO

on important things, forget it. He's half butterfly, half donkey, that's what he is.

As a three, what we do is completely different. Carl's the new one – he ought to be like a guest – but from the minute he's in, he takes over. One by one, he ruins or turns us against all the games we used to like (see fig. 6).

It's hard to say exactly what we do instead. We wander around more. Often we just go to the shopping centre and look at stuff, talking about what we'd buy if we had a million pounds. It sounds boring, but with Carl we're never bored. There are lots of things I don't like about him, but I can never say he's boring.

the playground

When term starts, I get the best news ever. Carl isn't at our school. During the week, it's going to be just me and Olly again, like before. And I've got a plan. I'm going to be better to Olly. I'm not going to boss him around or ever tell him he's stupid.

It'll have to be gradual. It can't look like I'm sucking up. But slowly, I'll win him back and show him that we don't need Carl.

First day back at school is more exciting than you'd ever dare admit, not just because it always is, but because we're starting the last year of primary. It's like being royalty. At long last, we're the biggest. We're in charge.

During first playtime, everyone gathers at the best bit of territory, around the water fountain. You only get this spot when you're the top year, and none of us has ever really been here before, except to dash in and get a ball, or after school hours, which doesn't count.

From here, there's a view of the whole playground, no one can sneak up behind you, and you have command of the best football pitch, which for now we're not even using. There's too much to get used to. No one wants to play just yet.

The girls in our year have now got the very top of the hilly bit, under the tree. A couple of the boys go over to talk to them and check out their new land. We all watch as they do it. It's a strange thing to attempt, but it's not one of the saddos or girly boys who does it. It's Martin Kaye and Scott Franklin. So instead of laughing at them for talking to girls, everyone just watches, impressed.

The girls are a bit frosty, but let them have a look round. Then Martin and Scott try and persuade Verity to come back and have a look at where the boys are, but she won't. You can see by the gestures what they're saying. She screams when Martin tries to pull her up from where she's sitting, but you can tell she likes it. Verity's the prettiest girl in the school. Martin bought her a Mr Whippy on the last day of term, before the summer holidays, so everyone knows she's taken.

Whatever Martin and Scott do, you can't laugh at. Martin's captain of the football team and he's had a trial at Watford. Scott's dad's a fireman. If anyone else was wearing the trousers they are, it would be the biggest joke of the day. They don't go straight down, but get narrower and narrower all the way to the ankles, almost like tights. Because it's Martin and Scott, no one says a word. Apparently, they're called drainpipes. You'd never guess they were for boys.

Our new classroom's upstairs, which is excellent, and our teacher's Mrs Dickson, which isn't is as bad as it could be. She's got bug eyes and is quite strict, but at least she's not Mr Hughes.

Me and Olly get ourselves the perfect desk, right at the side, near the windows, two rows in from the back.

She says we're going to do the whole history of everything, starting with the Egyptians. This happens every year, and I've never got past the Romans, except once when Miss Wood did *Henry VIII*. One Friday, Miss Wood came to school with a surfboard on her roof rack because she was going on a trip with her boyfriend. She was amazing.

the shopping centre

It's Saturday afternoon. Me, Olly and Carl are hanging around under the statue of Sally the skipping girl in the centre of town. It's got benches all round it, so everyone can sit there looking up at where Sally's knickers would be if her skirt wasn't solid metal.

We're not doing much. Carl's drinking a Slush Puppy and Olly's stuck into a Curly Wurly, but I'm just sitting there. When I see Rachel and Lucy walking towards us, at first I'm not too worried. I don't have to say hello to her in public because there's no way she'd say hello to me. There's always the chance that she'll look at me and pull a face as she walks past, but the probability of the other two noticing isn't very high. I don't know how it came about, and neither of us had to say anything, but for a long time it's been agreed that pretending not to know each other is the safest policy in front of other people. It's like a peace treaty (see fig. 7).

As she and Lucy get closer, there's something about the way they're walking that gives me the heebie-jeebies. They're not heading up to the shopping centre or going on to McDonald's, they're coming straight at us. It's not dead straight, since their balance isn't very good because they hook their arms together when they walk, as if they're trying to pretend they're one four-legged animal. They practically are, as well.

By the time Rachel and Lucy are a few metres away, it's

FIGURE 7.

HOW TO BEHAVE IN PUBLIC WITH RACHEL: TERMS OF THE PEACE TREATY

ACCEPTABLE

CATCHING THE EYE

NODDING

PULLING A FACE

IGNORING

PRETENDING TO BE DEAF

SMILING (BUT NOT IF ANYONE SEES)

UNACCEPTABLE

SPEAKING

COMING TOO CLOSE

PASSING ITEMS FROM ONE TO THE OTHER

POINTING

obvious they're coming towards me. Carl and Olly are staring at them, and I'm dreading what's going to happen next. I don't know what it's going to be, but there has to be a reason why Rachel's coming to talk to me, and that reason has to be bad.

You know how it goes dark just before it buckets with rain? That's how I feel.

But she comes right up to me, then walks past, and stops in front of Carl. 'You're Chainsaw Boy, aren't you?' she says.

He looks up at her, and takes an extra long time to answer. 'Who's asking?' he says.

'You attacked my dad with a chainsaw, didn't you?'

Carl looks at me, and back at Rachel, then he does it again, checking us out – brother and sister.

'I never attacked him,' he says, eventually.

'Yes, you did,' she says.

'No, I didn't.'

He's got a funny look. It's not the funny look he gets if I contradict him, it's a different funny look. He's smiling and not smiling at the same time. You can see right into his eyes, big and blue and clear.

'You did. I saw.'

'I wasn't attacking him.'

'What were you doing, then?'

Carl takes ages to answer. It's not like he's trying to think of what to say, though. He's just making them wait.

'I was showing him how it works, wasn't I.'

Rachel and Lucy both crack up laughing. But they don't take their eyes off him. They toss their hair around for ages to get it back to where it was before they started laughing, then Lucy pipes up. 'Rachel wants to know if you're a psycho.'

He doesn't even flinch. 'Maybe I want to know if she's a psycho,' he says. The way he's talking, you'd think he was a different person. His voice is all sweet and he's got a little smirk at the corner of his mouth that I've never seen before.

'Well, she's not,' says Lucy.

'And I'm supposed to take your word for it, am I?' he says.

Rachel whispers something to Lucy, and they walk off, but after a couple of steps they stop and turn round.

'How old are you?' asks Rachel.

Me and Olly both stare at Carl. We've never asked. It's because we think he's older than us but, if he tells us he's older, it'll make things different. It'll mean he can tell us what to do more. But it'll also do the opposite because, if he is older, it makes him a bit of a saddo that he isn't with people his own age. It's better to leave it unsaid.

'How old are *you*?' he says.

'Thirteen.' They both answer together.

'Me, too,' he says.

'What are you doing with them, then?' Rachel says, flapping a hand at me and Olly without even looking at us.

'Babysitting, aren't I,' he says.

They both stare at Carl out of the edges of their eyes, taking him in like he's a plate of food they might eat or might throw away.

'Want some Slush Puppy?'

He tilts his straw at them. This is a record. Carl offering someone something.

'What flavour is it?' asks Lucy. She's a bit fat.

'Blue,' he says.

'That's not a flavour.'

'Yes, it is.'

'It's a colour.'

'It's both.'

'No such thing.'

'What's orange, then?'

'Clever dick,' says Rachel.

'Smartypants,' says Lucy.

Then the two of them run away. Literally, run. It's embarrassing. It's like they're seven.

'You're thirteen?' I say.

'No.' He's not even looking at me. He's watching Rachel and Lucy head up to the shopping centre.

'You told them you were.'

'Well done, deaf aid.'

'But you're not?'

He shrugs.

'You twelve?'

He shrugs again.

'Eleven?'

'Let's go after them,' he says.

'No way.'

'Stay here, then. I don't care.'

Then he's up and off, following Rachel and Lucy.

Me and Olly sit there for a bit. There's no way I'm following my own sister around a shopping centre on a Saturday afternoon. Absolutely no way.

Olly's had proof about the chainsaw story now. He can't still tell me it's a lie. I'm trying to think of a non-gloaty way to point this out, when Olly stands up and runs after Carl.

Sitting there on my own, I feel like a total idiot. There's still a whole afternoon to go. If I let Carl and Olly leave me out, it'll be the beginning of them doing it more and more often. I know that's what Carl wants. He wants to cut me out. I don't even think it's because he likes Olly more than me or because he thinks he'll have more fun without me. It's just that he's trying to beat me. And if he gets rid of me, that's how he'll know he's won.

I swivel in my seat, and I can see Olly's hair straight away. Him and Carl are just going up the steps into the shopping centre. Before I know it, I'm running after them.

I find them in Dixons. Carl's pretending to look at TVs, but is actually staring out of the window at the entrance to Chelsea Girl over the way. Olly's gazing at the different piles of blank tapes, and you can tell from the way his lips are moving that he's trying to work out how much cheaper a five-pack is. He does this every time we go into Dixons. Olly's tortured about the difference between a D90, an AD90 and an AR90. He has a personality crisis every time he buys a blank tape, and that's before you even factor in the single, three-pack, five-pack problem. He used to agonize over the sixty *versus* ninety thing, too, but he's got over that now. Olly's dad's got a tape-to-tape with high-speed dubbing. You can turn the volume up while it's going, and it sounds like mice singing. Olly's the taping guru because of his dad's stereo.

'Let's go,' Carl barks.

We turn, and he's already out the door.

When we catch up with him, he sticks out an arm to hold us back, and puts a finger to his lips. He points up ahead, and we can see Rachel and Lucy not far in front, doing their leany walk across the marble floor.

We follow them all the way to Etam. They go in, and Carl spins us all round to face the nearest shop, two down from where Rachel and Lucy are. The three of us pretend to look in the window, which is stupid, because it's a jeweller's, and we're looking at a display of wedding rings.

'This is boring,' I say.

'Shut up,' says Carl.

'What are we standing here for?' I say.

'Because I want to.'

'Let's go.'

'Shut up whingeing.'

'Bloody 'ell!' says Olly. 'That one's three hundred pounds!'

We're there for ages, long enough to buy ten years' worth of clothes, but when Rachel and Lucy come out they aren't even carrying anything. That's when they see us. Or Carl, anyway.

Lucy spots him first, looks away, whispers something to Rachel, then they both look, and rush off.

'They've seen us,' I say. 'Let's go.'

But Carl's already gone after them. Then Olly, too. I don't have an option. I have to go, following my sister around the shopping centre. This is the bleakest day of my life.

Rachel and Lucy duck into the Body Shop, and Carl goes right in after them. This is one step too far for me and Olly. We just hover in the doorway, watching. Rachel and Lucy go round the whole shop, like they've never seen any of it before, spraying, dabbing, sniffing and wiping little patches of things on the back of their hands. Carl does the same, but only in the bit of the shop with soaps and shampoo. He's not really looking at any of it, though, he's just watching the girls. He doesn't even pretend he isn't. Every time they look up they see him staring at them, which makes them just concentrate harder on the bottles and tubes in their hands, but you can tell they're not really thinking about shopping, either.

There's a spot where the women's stuff joins the men's stuff, and the three of them get there at the same time. They stop staring, and for a moment it looks like they've never met. Then Rachel sprays a tester right at Carl's head, and the two girls crack up, dump everything and run right out of the shop. They go past us as if we're invisible, so close that the stink of them makes my nose itch. Between them they're wearing every tester in the shop. Carl's after them straight away, running, and he also pretends we're not there.

The girls head straight for the escalator that goes up to the food hall. Carl's right behind them.

Me and Olly stand there in the door of the Body Shop for ages, not speaking.

Rachel, Lucy and Carl have long since disappeared from sight when Olly says, 'Shall we see what's happened?'

It doesn't feel like following any more. It's just curiosity. I nod, and we walk slowly to the escalator. We go all the way up in silence, just letting it carry us even though there's no one in front to stop us walking.

The food court's mostly empty. We can't see them anywhere. We do a big circle, all the way round, before we get to the corner where the emergency exits are and see the three of them, in the most hidden table of the whole place, sitting together with an ice cream each.

Lucy looks a bit embarrassed, but the other two just stare at us crossly. It's as if they've got a word each stamped on their foreheads: 'GO' on Carl's and 'AWAY' on Rachel's. By the way Olly's shifting from foot to foot, I can tell he just wants to turn and leave. That's the worst thing we could do, though. We mustn't let Carl and Rachel humiliate us.

I can't stare for long, or they'll think I'm upset.

'Let's get some chips,' I say, just to Olly, but in a voice that everyone can hear. Chips are more grown-up than ice cream.

We get them from the burger counter and sit at a table on the other side of the hall, too far away for them to think we're watching, but close enough to see what's going on. I make sure it's me facing away from them and Olly towards. He keeps me posted, but there's nothing to report except that they just carry on talking.

Long after we've finished our chips, we're in the middle of

making sugar patterns on the table when suddenly there's a huff of air, sugar granules are all over the place and Carl's sitting at our table, smiling his wonky smile.

'All right?' he says.

I look round and the girls have disappeared.

carl's house

On the way back from the shopping centre no one speaks much. Even Olly realizes that Carl's gone too far.

Both of us being cross with him is a first. I have to do something with it, before it goes away, but I can't think how to turn Olly's anger into anything useful. I just know it's an opportunity. A chance to tip the balance back towards me.

It happens in wrestling all the time, when one guy is beating up the other guy, but he gets too cocky and starts showing off, and makes a mistake, and the guy who was losing suddenly switches it round and beats up the guy who up until then was winning. Dad laughs at it and says it's all a fix, but he doesn't understand. You can learn everything you need to know from wrestling.

Carl's trying to chat as we wander home, but neither me or Olly is answering properly. He can't just ignore us one minute, then try and be our friend the next. He can't take sides with my sister against me. That's not how things work. Even Olly knows that.

Then I get an idea. 'Let's go to your house, Carl,' I say.

He gives me a quick, sharp look. We've never been there, not once. Carl's always acted like it's not an option. It's one of those houses you can tell from the street doesn't get any visitors. If you had a paper round, you'd want to skip it.

Carl pretends I haven't said anything.

When we get to the corner where it's one way to Olly's and

another way to Carl's and mine, Carl keeps on going to Olly's, like normal. I stop, and Olly stops with me, which is a good sign. It feels great to have Olly there, next to me, starting something against Carl.

'I thought we were going to yours,' I say.

'Why d'you think that?'

'You didn't say no.'

'I didn't say yes.'

'So let's go, then.'

'I don't want to.'

'Why not?'

'I just don't.'

'Why not?'

'I just don't.'

'What if Olly doesn't want you to go to his?'

'Who says he doesn't?'

'Olly does.'

'Says you.'

'Says him.'

'Yeah?'

'Yeah.'

'Yeah?'

'Yeah. Isn't that right?'

We both turn to Olly. He's standing there, not looking at either of us.

'You want to go to Carl's, don't you?' I say.

He looks at me, then at Carl, then at me, then at the ground. He nods.

'See?' I say.

'Why are you such a baby?' says Carl.

I shrug. He's just trying to change the subject.

'I'm going home,' Carl says. 'This is boring.'

'You not inviting us?' I say.

'No.'

'What if we come anyway?'

'You can't,' he says.

'What if we follow you?'

He steps right up to me, close as someone who's about to give you a kiss. He looks right into my eyes, not blinking. 'You wouldn't dare.'

'You reckon?' I say. I try not to blink, but I can't do it. I end up blinking twice as much as normal.

'Yeah, I reckon,' he says. And without looking back, he slowly walks home.

We watch him for a bit, ambling away, and part of me just wants to give up, but I make myself hit Olly on the arm and say, 'Come on.'

We cross the road after Carl and duck into the driveway of the first house on the block. I poke my head out and watch until Carl goes round the corner into my street. We jump out and sprint for it, right to the corner, then we pin ourselves against a fence and peek round.

Carl's still walking home, not waiting to ambush us, or even turning to see if we're behind. His walk's more of a lollop than usual, and he's scuffing his heels on the ground with each step.

When he's way ahead, we sneak up a few houses and duck into a driveway. We have to do it in stages, sprinting then waiting, so if he turns round he probably won't see us. We don't really have to do it at all, since we know where his house is, and we know he's going there, but that's beside the point. It feels right to be tailing him.

He doesn't turn round once. By the time we get to his house, we reckon it's about 50/50 whether he knew we were following and ignored us, or whether we did the whole thing unnoticed.

Standing in the drive of Carl's neighbour, with him disappeared inside, we don't know what to do next. If we want to prove a point, we have to ring the doorbell and tell him we've come to visit. That's what we threatened to do. Just following him home then chickening out doesn't achieve anything. We might as well not have bothered. Except that up close, with the scary, flaky house right there in front of us, neither me or Olly feels like seeing it through. There's something about the way the curtains are all closed, or about the heaps of stinky bags where the bin ought to be, that makes you not want to go in.

A light goes on upstairs, which is probably Carl's room, but could be someone else's. After a while, it feels strange to be standing there in Carl's neighbour's driveway, not doing anything except spying.

'Are we gonna do it?' says Olly. It's not a challenge, it's just a question, but I don't want to be the one that admits to bottling it.

'S'pose so.'

'Go on, then.'

'We're doing it together.'

'I know.'

If there was a record for the slowest walk ever up a front path, we would have won it. We keep on stopping, staring at each other, then almost scarpering, but not. Even when we get right up to the door it's ages before either of us rings. Just touching the bell without even pressing it makes us feel funny, and both of us has to try several times before I finally manage to give it a proper push. Even after that we're within one twitch of running for it.

There are loads of locks which clunk and slide before the door swings open. But it's not Carl. It's a woman. His mum. It's normal, really, that she should answer the door of her own house, but neither of us is prepared for it to be anyone other than Carl, and the sight of her makes me instantly regret what we've done.

Her face is all made up for a party that looks as if it happened days ago. She's wearing black leggings and a baggy white T-shirt which says 'RELAX' on it in huge letters. You don't normally notice what someone's wearing. It's only when it looks wrong that people's clothes stand out, and there's definitely something wrong about Carl's mum. She's dressed like she's going out from the neck up and staying in from the neck down.

Her hair's all bouffed up, except for one side where she's probably slept on it. At first she looks right over our heads, and it takes a moment for her to look down and see us. When she does, she peers into our faces as if she can't tell whether she's supposed to know who we are. There's something strange about the slow way she looks at us, with a shiny stillness in her eyes like someone playing dead.

I really wish we'd never rung the bell now, but it's too late to turn back. 'We're Carl's friends,' I say.

'Carl's friends?' She says it oddly, like the two words don't match.

'We came round to . . . to visit. To see if he's in, I mean.'

'To visit Carl?' Then the penny drops, and her face completely changes. She flaps her arm and gives a huge, lipsticky smile. 'Oh, come in, come in. That's so sweet. That's so *sweet*. Come in. Come *in*. Come through.'

She leads us down the hall and into the living room. The house is identical to mine. The shape of the rooms and where all the doors and windows are. I could walk round the whole place blindfold. It could be my home. Except the feel of it isn't right. From the moment we're inside, I can sense that something's not right.

Even though they've been in the street months, it looks like they just moved in. The only furniture is a velvety, dark blue sofa in the corner and a TV on a cardboard box in the middle of the floor. On top of the telly there's a tin of baked beans with a spoon sticking out of it. A heap of dining chairs is slumped in one corner, stacked up, half of them upside-down. There's nothing on the walls except old wallpaper, with faded shapes where the previous owners must have had their shelves. The only light is from a single bulb above the TV, which is too bright to look at, but still leaves the room grey and murky. Even though it's daytime, the curtains are shut, hanging in sags so you can see U-shapes of sky through gaps in the top.

It doesn't smell right, either. There's something a bit sicky, a bit sweet in the air. And it's hot. Weirdly hot. You can hear the radiators shushing to themselves.

Suddenly Carl's mum seems really excited, as if the two of us turning up is some kind of special occasion. 'Would you . . . would you like . . . some squash?' she asks. 'Orange squash.'

It's years since I drank squash, but I say yes anyway. It seems like the safest answer. Olly says yes, too.

'Right,' she says. 'Squash. Two squashes.'

She goes into the kitchen through a little arch, and we watch her opening and shutting cupboards, slowly at first, then faster and faster, banging them open and shut, round and round the kitchen, doing each cupboard two, then three times, saying over and over again to herself, 'Squash-squash-squash-squash-squash.'

Every now and then she stops, looks up at us, and says, 'I'm sure I had some. I've definitely got some.'

Her hair's getting more and more straggly, and her face is getting redder, as she keeps on going through her cupboards, shifting tins and jars and bottles backwards and forwards, looking in the same places again and again.

'Can we just have juice instead?' I say.

She looks at me as if I've broken into the house, as if I've just appeared without warning, then her face suddenly brightens again and she says, 'Yes – juice. Juice-juice. We have juice.'

She opens the fridge, and it's completely empty. There's a tub of margarine in there and a jar of mayonnaise, but that's it. She stares in, like she's amazed by the emptiness. Like she's been robbed.

'Or water,' says Olly. 'Just water'd be good.'

'Water!' she says. 'Water-water. We have that.'

She gives it to us in chunky, cut-glass tumblers, the outside dripping wet from the tap and a bit sticky. Neither of us wants to drink any, but she's staring at us, so we have to.

'Very nice,' says Olly, trying to be polite.

This is water he's talking about. It's the stupidest thing Olly's ever said and, if I wasn't so freaked out by Carl's mum, I'd probably wet myself laughing. As it is, I don't even smile, I just try and remember it for later.

'What are your names?' she asks.

'I'm Ben.'

She takes a couple of steps towards me, curls up her hand and gives my cheek two strokes with the back of her fingers, like I'm her cat or her boyfriend. 'Very nice to meet you, Ben . . . And you are?'

'Olly,' he says, taking a step back.

She shuffles forward and pats him a couple of times on the top of his head.

'What wonderful hair,' she says. 'Is it from your mother's side or your father's?'

'Er . . . Mum, I suppose.'

'Well, she must be very beautiful.'

Olly shrugs and wrinkles his nose.

'I've dyed mine once too often,' she says, fingering her hair like she's pulling fluff out of a carpet. 'It'll never be the same again.'

She sighs, as if she's getting bored, then her face suddenly comes alive with a new idea. 'Shall I get Carl?' she says, all excited.

I want to say, 'No need,' or something funny that would make the place seem less spooky, but I don't dare, and just nod.

She doesn't go out to the stairs, but just stands where she is, tilts her head back and shouts up at the living-room ceiling. 'CARL! CARL!'

She raises her eyebrows and tilts her head on one side while we all wait for an answer, but there's nothing.

'COME DOWN, CARL,' she shouts. 'YOUR FRIENDS ARE HERE!'

There's still no answer, but you can hear an instant thump, then rapid footsteps.

'So . . .' she says, as if starting a sentence will help her think of something to say. 'Are you . . . at the unit with Carl?'

'The unit?'

'Are you friends of his from the unit? He's been moaning that the other boys are . . . are weirdos, or some other word, but you both seem very nice.'

'We're . . . we're just neighbours,' I say.

Then Carl appears in the doorway, and when he sees us his

face goes completely still. You can tell he's angry, but it's not like a normal person getting angry. This is something different.

'What are you doing here?' he says quietly. It's scarier than if he'd shouted it.

'We just thought we'd pop in,' I say. My voice is shaking a bit, now.

'I told you not to come,' he says.

'Carl!' says his mum.

Then there's the sound of a key in the door. Carl's mum jolts and stiffens, as if she's been prodded. She swivels her head, stares at the mess in the kitchen, then dashes in and starts frantically putting things back into cupboards and rinsing glasses.

'Into the garden,' says Carl. Before we even know what's happening, he's shoved us to the back door and out.

Outside, Carl won't look at us. You can't tell if he's angry or ashamed or upset or anything. For the first time ever, he looks weak. Just from the way he's standing, you can tell he isn't going to have a go at us.

More than ever, I wish we weren't there.

The grass is up to our knees. I can tell from all the huge, straggly plants that the garden used to be a proper one, but isn't any more. In the far corner is a droopy, old tree. Carl walks over to it, not letting us see his face. He starts picking up rotting apples off the ground near the trunk and splatting them at the fence. He does a few, then he just stops and stands there.

For a moment, I think he might be about to cry, and I realize that the idea of him crying is more scary than anything else he could do. I'd rather he screamed at us. I'd rather he started a fight.

Part of me knows I should go over to where he's standing

and say something to cheer him up. But what I really want to do is chuck a big, rotten apple right into his face and tell him to piss off and leave Olly and me alone for good. If there was ever a moment to get rid of him, this is it.

'She's nice, your mum,' says Olly. 'Very friendly.'

Without moving his body, Carl turns his head and stares at Olly like he's a total idiot. There's a long silence.

'What's the unit?' I say.

He doesn't answer.

'What is it?' I say. 'The unit.'

He's looking at me as if, but still he won't answer.

'Is it where you go to school? Is it instead of school?'

Olly's staring at me as if I've gone mad. Carl doesn't move and doesn't speak, but his breath's getting faster, and you can see the energy coiling up tighter and tighter inside him. Something's about to snap. He's either going to sit down right there and cry, or he's going to go mental. I know I should stop, but I can't.

'Is it a special school?' I say. 'Did you get sent there?'

'Shut up, Ben,' says Olly.

'Is it a special school for nutters?' I say.

'I'm going,' says Olly. He turns and marches to the back door, but just stands there, watching us, not leaving.

'That's why you're not at our school, isn't it?' I say. 'You're not at Mountview. You're at a loony-bin school.'

Carl bends over, picks up an apple and chucks it at my head. I duck, and it just misses. Then another one comes. And another. They fly right past me and into a bush, so I've got nothing to pick up and throw back. Then one hits me smack on the cheek and explodes in a mouldy, brown pulp. It stings my face like I've been slapped, and I can't see anything.

I sense that he's coming towards me, but I can't properly tell what he's holding. It looks long and straight, and he's got it raised above his head.

When it cracks down against my skull I can feel that it's something narrow but hard. I can't see properly to defend myself, and the thing's flying at my face, zipping towards me with the sound of air being ripped. It's a stick of bamboo. It hits my ear, then my cheek, and the only thing I can do is curl up in a ball on the grass, while it comes down again and again on my back.

Carl only stops when Olly jumps at him and pushes him over, barging into him with a shoulder, and as soon as there's a moment I get up and run for it, with Olly following. We race through the house, not even looking at Olly's mum and the man who came in, and sprint out of the front door and down the street, running all the way, only stopping outside my house.

We stand there, doubled over, straining to get our breath back. Just being out of Carl's house, and away from him, feels like being let off school early. I'm grinning, my body tingling with relief, and it's a while before I realize Olly isn't smiling back. He's staring at me.

'You're bleeding,' he says.

'I'd better go in.'

I don't, though. I just stand with Olly, in the middle of the road, looking at him. There's something missing. I have to know what he thinks. I reckon I might have won him back. We could be back to normal now. But I need to hear it from him. Something in his face means I can't be sure until Olly says it.

'He's crazy,' I say.

Olly doesn't answer. He turns away and gazes down the street, back towards Carl's house.

'He totally lost it,' I say.

Olly still won't look at me.

'If you hadn't saved me . . .'

'You made him do it,' he says.

'No, I didn't. He's a nutcase. Why d'you think he's at that school?'

Olly doesn't answer for ages, then mutters, 'You made him do it.'

'Can't you think of anything else to say?' I'm angry, now. Not with Carl. With Olly.

He just shrugs. 'You don't know what it's like,' he says, eventually.

'What what's like?'

He shrugs again, staring at the ground.

'What what's like?'

'I'm going home,' he says, and walks off.

He stays in the middle of the road, not looking back, as he wanders away. Near the corner, he does a little jump and kicks a stone, which pings against the side of a car.

my room

When I catch sight of myself in the hall mirror, all bloody and appley, I understand why Olly was staring. It makes *me* stare, and it's my face. But I can't stand there for long. I have to get washed and changed before anyone sees me, or there'll be questions.

I go straight upstairs, and I'm just going past the toilet when Donny comes out and sees me. At first he looks right through me, like normal, then he does a double take and grabs my arm to stop me getting away.

I wriggle free and run for my bedroom, but I can't get the door shut in time. He shoves his foot in so I'm just pushing against his shoe. It's useless. Usually he's only in socks, and I'd be able to crunch him into submission, but today he's got his DMs on.

Then the door starts to push back. I keep him out for maybe ten seconds, then my feet slip and he's in. This is typical of Donny. The only time I don't want his attention is when I get it.

He looks at my face, and gives a little wince. He reaches out to touch it, but I slap his hand away. He's between me and the door, so I can't escape.

'You OK?' he says.

Just him asking that makes me almost start to cry, and I have to sit down on the edge of my bed. Donny being nice wasn't what I expected. The shock of it undoes all my defences.

'Who was it?' he says. He sounds angry.

I just shake my head.

'Who was it?'

'No one,' I say, my voice wobbling.

He sits down next to me, and puts his arm round my shoulders. It feels strange at first, but then I'm glad he's there. I can't remember the last time he touched me friendlily. It's probably when I was a baby. I try not to cry, and just about manage it.

Just when I'm getting used to the idea of Donny being nice, he gets up and walks out without saying anything. I hear a tap go on and off, then he comes back with a damp flannel and sits back down next to me.

'You can't tell Mum,' I say.

'This might hurt,' he says, and he starts to dab at the apple and blood on my face. My hands are trembling now, and I sit on them so Donny won't notice. I can't help wincing when Donny touches the cut on my cheek, but he's being as gentle as he can. Twice he goes back to the bathroom and rinses out the flannel.

Every so often, he tells me I'm being brave, which isn't something he's ever said before.

When it's done, he says again, quietly, 'Who was it?'

I shake my head.

'Was it the boy from down the road?'

'It was an accident,' I say.

'It was him?'

'We were just playing.'

'What did he hit you with?'

'We were just mucking around.'

'So you're playing with him now? He's your friend?'

'We don't *play* with him. But we do stuff with him. Me and Olly.'

'You, Olly and him. You're friends?'

'Yeah.'

'Since when?'

I shrug.

'Don't be an idiot, Ben. He's a bad kid. He's crazy. If you play with him, this is going to happen again.'

'We don't *play*.'

'Sorry.' He smirks for a moment, then his face goes dead serious again. 'That boy's bad. He's not right in the head.'

'He's my friend.'

'He beat you up.'

'I got him, too. I said things.'

Donny shakes his head, then takes one of my shoulders in each hand and turns me towards him. I feel tiny with him looming over me, staring down, looking me straight in the eye. 'Do you want me to get him back?' he says.

I don't reckon Donny's ever been in a fight in his life but, from the way he says it, you know he means it. He'd really do it.

It's an exciting thought. I can see it happening, in my imagination, and it looks great. Donny's standing over him, twice his size, and he's punching Carl all over, and it's so easy for him it's not even fun. He's hitting him again and again with a totally calm expression on his face, and I'm watching from the other side of the road. It's right outside our house. Carl's shouting to me, his face all twisted and red, begging me to make Donny stop, and I'm just standing there with my arms folded, taking it in, saying nothing.

'No,' I say. 'Don't.'

He stands and walks to the door. 'Get cleaned up,' he says. 'Have a bath.'

'You won't say anything, will you?'

He shakes his head. 'Won't make any difference. Unless you wear a balaclava for a week.'

I go to the bathroom mirror and look at the mark on my cheek, which is long and slightly lumpy – part cut, part bruise. I touch it with my little finger, and it zings with a pain that hurts but makes me want to do it again.

I lock the door, and turn the bath on full. We've got old-fashioned taps that come out in a big, steamy gush.

By dinner I've got my story straight. Sword fight with sticks in Olly's garden and he got me by accident. They swallow the whole thing. They don't even notice the way me and Donny are looking at each other.

through rachel's wall

It's a while before I see Carl again or even hear his name. Me and Olly stop talking about him. It's like the whole thing never happened.

He even disappears from the street. I never see him or his mum anywhere. Their car* changes position outside his house, so I know they're around, coming and going, but I never catch sight of them. That doesn't mean much, though. They've never been people you see walking around. Carl's dad doesn't even live there. Or if he does, he's the Invisible Man.

So it's just me and Olly again. But it's nothing like it was before Carl turned up. It feels strange. Without him, everything seems a bit aimless, a bit flat. We don't quite know what to do any more.

Before Carl, me and Olly just played. We were into games, mainly. But it feels like we've grown out of that now. Trouble is, the other stuff – the stuff that comes next, the stuff that isn't really doing anything, but is just hanging out and walking round the shopping centre and seeing what turns up – that's all totally boring without Carl. Because nothing turns up. He was the one who made things happen.

Even though we don't mention him, his absence is always

* A gold Ford Capri (with a spoiler) that would look cool if it ever got washed and if it didn't have a crunched-in headlight. It would be exciting to be in a car crash, but only a small one.

89

with us, like an extra person in the room. Perhaps that's why neither of us wants to say his name, because it feels as if he's still there, changing what we do and what we say, sitting on our shoulders and whispering to us about what's childish and what isn't.

I don't miss him. I wouldn't want him back. But when I sense that Olly's missing him, or is thinking about him, that's when I feel bad. That's when I feel I'm not good enough, or interesting enough, or fun enough, and that's when I partly wish he'd come back because, if he did, all those stupid thoughts would just go away. We'd never be bored again. And it's only when we're bored that I think Olly doesn't like me as much as he used to.

Then one evening I'm in my room doing homework, and a row breaks out downstairs. It sounds like a big one, but I can't hear what they're saying. Next thing, Rachel's running upstairs and slamming the door to her room. Mum's right behind and barges straight in to carry on the row. You can tell who's doing what just by the sound of the footsteps and door slams. Everyone has their own personal signature when it comes to slamming doors.

They start up again in Rachel's room, and it's right through the wall from mine so I can hear every word.

'Don't run away from me, Rachel,' Mum says. 'I told you you're not to see him again.'

'I'LL SEE WHO I WANT!'

Volume-wise, Rachel's about double Mum.

'Not while you're living in my house.'

'THEN I'LL GO SOMEWHERE ELSE.'

'You can't, Rachel. You're thirteen.'

'WELL, YOU'RE A FASCIST.'

'There's a lot of things you don't understand yet, Rachel.'

'WELL, THERE'S A MILLION THINGS YOU DON'T UNDERSTAND AND NEVER WILL.'

After a long gap, Mum says, 'What, Rachel? What don't I understand?'

'EVERYTHING.'

'Like what?'

'LIKE I LOVE HIM.'

'Don't say that.'

'I DO.'

'You don't, Rachel. You don't know what it means.'

'*YOU* DON'T KNOW WHAT IT MEANS. YOU DON'T CARE ABOUT ME. YOU DON'T CARE ABOUT ANYONE. YOU JUST WANT TO TELL ME WHAT TO DO.'

'I'm telling you what to do for a reason, Rachel. He's a very troubled boy. He's not someone a person like you should get involved with.'

'BECAUSE HE'S TROUBLED?'

'Yes.'

'WELL, YOU'RE A NICE PERSON, AREN'T YOU? STEER CLEAR OF ANYONE WHO'S IN ANY TROUBLE. DON'T LET YOURSELF BE NICE TO SOMEONE WHO ISN'T 100 PER CENT HAPPY. THAT'S A REALLY GOOD ATTITUDE, ISN'T IT? THANKS, MUM, FOR HELPING ME BE A GOOD PERSON – FOR SHARING YOUR BRILLIANT WISDOM.'

'I'm not talking about him being unhappy. You know I don't mean that. What I'm talking about is that he's dangerous.'

'NOT WITH ME, HE ISN'T. HE'S VERY GENTLE.'

'He's dangerous, Rachel. You saw what he nearly did to Dad.'

Now I know for sure who they're talking about. I sensed it

from the start, but this is when I give up hoping it might be someone else. Rachel and Carl. Girlfriend and boyfriend. It's gross.

'HE'S NOT REALLY LIKE THAT.'

'If he can do that once, without any provocation, he can do it again.'

'WHO SAYS THERE WAS NO PROVOCATION?'

'Oh, so that whole thing was Dad's fault, was it?'

'MAYBE IT WAS. WE DON'T KNOW WHAT HE SAID. IF I HAD A CHAINSAW, I'D WANT TO CUT HIM UP HALF THE TIME.'

'You're being ridiculous now, Rachel.'

'WELL, I DON'T CARE WHAT YOU SAY, I'M NOT GOING TO STOP SEEING HIM.'

'In that case, you're grounded. You're not going to see anyone.'

'MUM! THERE'S NOTHING WRONG WITH HIM. YOU'RE JUST A TOTAL SNOB!'

'This is nothing to do with snobbery, Rachel. He's unbalanced. His mother's a drunk. His father's God knows where . . .'

'SHE'S NOT A DRUNK. YOU DON'T EVEN KNOW HER.'

'She is, Rachel.'

'YOU'LL SAY ANYTHING TO MAKE ME DO WHAT YOU WANT, AND YOU MUST THINK I'M STUPID IF YOU THINK I'LL JUST BELIEVE YOU.'

'I know what's best for you, Rachel, and you're not to see him. He's a bad kid. He's completely out of control.'

'YOU CAN'T STOP ME.'

'Well, you can have a long, hard think, young lady, because you're not going out *at all* until you give me your word that you will *not* see that boy again. Understand?'

'THERE'S NO HUMAN RIGHTS IN THIS HOUSE. YOU'RE A COM-

PLETE NAZI. GET OUT OF MY ROOM. OR ARE YOU GOING TO TAKE MY ROOM AWAY FROM ME AS WELL?'

The door clicks shut, but it's a while before I hear Mum going back downstairs.

The house is noisy for a couple of weeks, Mum, Dad and Rachel either not speaking or going at each other like lunatics, sometimes even shouting about how they're not speaking, which makes no sense to me. She's supposedly grounded, but they can't actually stop her going out, and she won't tell them where she's going. That's what all the fuss is mainly about.

During this period, the average dinner-table conversation is something like the following (see fig. 8).

Then one day it's all silence. Strange, eerie, house-of-sickness silence. Rachel stops going out, she stops arguing with Mum and Dad, and she stops having visitors.

Even Lucy doesn't come any more.

When Rachel does leave her room, which is hardly ever, her eyes are all red and she won't speak. It's like someone's died. And they have. Rachelucy is no more.

Donny's watching *Open All Hours*, which I know he thinks is rubbish, so he's got no excuse for getting rid of me. If it was a different programme, I wouldn't stand a chance. I give him a nipple cripple to get his attention and start nagging him for an explanation of what's going on with Rachel. I'm not expecting an answer straight off, but I'm pretty confident I can wear him down.

He caves in relatively quickly, after a short (but one-sided) cushion fight and a prolonged double nipple-cripple revenge. Donny's the person you have to go to at times of family madness. He's the only one apart from me with any command of logic.

'Carl was her boyfriend,' he says.

'I know *that*,' I say.

FIGURE 8.

DINNER TABLE CONVERSATION DURING RACHEL STROP PERIOD

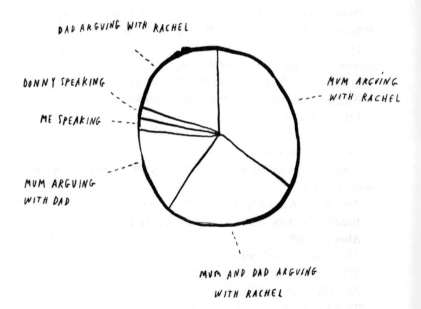

DAD ARGUING WITH RACHEL

DONNY SPEAKING

ME SPEAKING

MUM ARGUING WITH DAD

MUM ARGUING WITH RACHEL

MUM AND DAD ARGUING WITH RACHEL

'Even after all the arguments, after Mum and Dad said she had to break it off, she carried on seeing him, in secret. Then one day she went to see Lucy, and Carl was there, in her bedroom.'

'And?'

'That's it.'

'That's it?'

'Yes.'

'Can't be. What else?'

'There's nothing else. That's the story. She visited Lucy, and Carl was there. The end.'

I give this a long think.

'What were they doing?' I say.

Donny takes his eyes from the TV and looks at me, smirking. 'Who knows?' he says. 'What do you think they were doing?'

This is a tricky question. I can sense that just about any answer will make Donny laugh at me. I opt for a swerve.

'What do *you* think they were doing?' I say.

'Ahaaaa,' says Donny. 'I'll tell you if you tell me.'

'I think they were kissing,' I say. 'At least.'

'At least?' says Donny.

'Yeah. At least kissing.'

Donny smiles at me, but he doesn't laugh. 'I reckon you're right,' he says.

'And now Rachel doesn't want to see either of them again?'

'Exactly. Because they were both lying to her.'

'About what?'

'About seeing each other.'

'What – did they say they weren't?'

'No. They just never said they were.'

'That's not lying.'

'Yes it is.'

'No it isn't.'

'OK, it's not lying. It's cheating.'

'How's it cheating?'

'It just is.'

'How?'

'It just is.'

'Are there rules? Is there a rule book?'

'There's no book, but there are rules.'

'So how do you know what they are?'

'You just do.'

'How?'

'You figure them out.'

'How?'

'You just do.'

'So why's she upset?'

'I've already told you! I'm not explaining it again.'

Girls are weird. As you can see, Donny pretends to understand, but it all unravels if you question him. He doesn't get it any more than I do.

What's really mad is that it's all over the same boy I used to play with. Not *play*, but hang out with. And because I basically introduced them, it makes me feel ultra-mature to have such a major role in my sister getting her heart broken. When she's not too scary to talk to, I'll tell her I'm really sorry for the part I played in her suffering. I reckon she'll appreciate the gesture.

brent cross

The smaller the thing you want, the bigger the shop you have to go to. This is one of the strange rules of life that Mum lives by. You can get just about anything at our local shopping centre, but one day, when Mum decides she needs a few buttons, a whole excursion is planned, to Brent Cross.

Brent Cross is only shops – shops and a car park big enough to land a jumbo jet on – but going there is a Big Thing. Everyone has to be consulted. Everyone has to be invited. Lists have to be made. Cupboards have to be checked in all rooms for obscure items that might be missing, or broken, or just not bought yet.

It's hard to explain the excitement, really. I don't even like shops. But when Mum says she's going to Brent Cross, I can't not go. It would be like saying you didn't want to go on holiday.

Maybe it's because going there is the nearest you can get to time travel. You feel like you're going to spend the day in the future, where everything's paved over and roofed in and heated and perfect. Before you set off it feels like that, anyway. Once you're there it's always a letdown, but by then it's too late.

The other two aren't interested, so this time it's just me and Mum, which I know is a bit uncool, but secretly I quite like the idea of it. As we glide off the dual carriageway and down the spiral ramp that takes you to the car park, I can feel a little flutter of excitement in my chest. I know the trip will end up disappointing, but I've still got that thrill of arriving somewhere special, and of having Mum all to myself.

It's always my job to remember where the car is, and I try to fix it in my head, taking a mental photo of our spot. You can't rely on the cars around you because they might have gone by the time you leave, but I try and remember what they are anyway because it's interesting to know if they're still there when you come out. Maybe interesting is the wrong word, but you just want to know.

There's a red Mercedes next to us, and I make a secret bet with myself that it won't have left when we come back out because rich people have more money to spend, which must take longer.

Brent Cross doesn't have a front. Or if it does, we've never found it. We always just cross from the car park, go over one of those bobbly bits of pavement for blind people, then you get to a little door, and you go through it and straight away you're in the middle of racks of flouncy dresses for old women. Proper old women. Mum doesn't even look at them.

Our first stop is the button department of John Lewis. You wouldn't think there is one, but there is. Sometimes it's amazing how everything that exists is for sale somewhere.

All the buttons are heaped up in little perspex display cases, and they're amazingly fondlable. You just want to shove your hand into all of them and wiggle your fingers, and the great thing is, you can! The more you want to touch something, the more you won't be allowed, on the whole. But buttons are different, which is a good sign, because it always looked like this was a dead cert for being the most boring bit of the whole day, but we're doing it first, and already I'm having fun.

The number of things you can admit to enjoying is much lower than the number of things that are actually fun. Sliding your hand in a heap of slippery, cool buttons and having a good squelch is a classic example. You'd never tell anyone about that. I don't even know why I'm admitting it now.

There are some shops that only have women in. You feel cunning being there when you're not one – like a spy. Because I'm only a boy they forget about me, and I can listen to the things they say when they think there are no men listening. Most of it doesn't make sense, but I like hearing it anyway. I like the way women can make anything sound like a secret. I like the way their voices go when they're gossiping. Mum's stopped taking me into the changing rooms, though, which is a pity.

She's ages in the clothes section, but I don't really mind. Some days you get bored quickly, other days you're happy just watching people do things. I make a little fuss because she said she wasn't going to buy any clothes, but I only really do it to make sure she appreciates that I'm not making a big fuss.

'Don't tell Dad,' she says at the till. I think it's because she's bought too much stuff, but it's like there's a wink in her voice saying she doesn't really mean it.

'It's all very reduced,' she adds.

I shrug. She reaches out, smooths down a bit of my hair, and leaves her hand there, nestled into the back of my neck. Sometimes I hate it when she touches me and sometimes I like it. Today it's OK.

I can sense that after this I'm going to get a reward for being good. It's coffee and cake time. We call it that even though I have hot chocolate with an éclair, and Mum has tea and a croissant. I don't know why. That's just our name for it.

New school shoes are next on the list, which is something I dread and also kind of look forward to. It's the only time you get a grown-up down at your feet, anxiously questioning you about whether you feel comfortable, very comfortable or only slightly comfortable. In children's shoe shops, it's like the whole world's upside-down. The kids are the big experts, up high, giving information and opinions, while grown-ups crawl around on their hands and knees asking questions.

I specially like the bit where you have to walk to the door and back, with your mum and the sales assistant watching nervously for you to give your approval. When you get back, if you just give a slight 'Mmmm,' they look straight into your eyes and bark questions at you. 'Do they pinch? Do they slip? Do they squeeze? Rub? What is it?' And you can just be all laid back, and go 'Mmmm' again, like you're a king and you don't like what you've been given, but you can't even be bothered to explain why.

There's a catch, though. You end up with new shoes. And nothing's worse than new shoes. Wearing new shoes is like carrying round a placard saying: 'I'm a shiny, swotty pillock.' However hard you try, it's two weeks minimum to scuff them up and look normal again.

I'm just grateful that when I see the two of them, I've got the new shoes safely in a bag in my hand, and I'm wearing the old ones.

It's Olly and Carl. They're by the fountain, smoking.

I see them from miles away and stop dead. Mum stops, too, follows my stare, and sees who I've spotted. I can hardly believe it. The sight of them is like a kick in the stomach.

My first thought is that I have to get out of there as fast as I can, before they notice me. While I can act as if I don't know Olly still sees him, I'm in control of what happens next. It's my choice. But as soon as he knows I know, everything'll have to change. I'll have to make a stand. I'll have to walk away.

I can't just be the spare part. I'm not going to be the hanger-on to those two. I'd never do it and, even if I did, I'd know Carl was just waiting for a moment to turn on me and kick me out.

I have to get out of sight, but I can't. My legs won't budge. I'm stuck, staring at them, too shocked or upset or freaked out to get my body to go where I want.

'I'm going to give that boy a talking-to,' says Mum.

My head turns to her, and my jaw flops open. I'm so horrified by what she's said that I can't think of how to respond. I'd rather wear new shoes every day for the rest of my life than have Mum go over to them but, before I've even begun to explain to her that this will be the worst thing she's ever done to me, she's off, striding in their direction.

Now it's an emergency, my legs start working and I go after her.

'Don't,' I say.

'He's smoking,' she says.

'Please don't.'

She doesn't even break stride. We're getting closer now. They're going to see us. My whole world is seconds away from total collapse. I grab Mum's sleeve and dig my heels into the floor.

'MUM! DON'T!'

'Get off me.'

'DON'T! PLEEEEEASE!'

She can't move. I'm leaning right back and almost pulling her coat off. Then I turn my head, and see Olly and Carl. They must have heard me because now they're staring right at us, and I realize what I must look like: a screaming kid pulling at his mum's sleeve and having a tantrum like a five-year-old. This is the most humiliating thing ever.

I can't pull her back now, with them watching, so I let go. She shrugs her coat back on to her shoulder and, without even glancing at me, marches over to them. I can't follow. I can barely watch. I just want to curl up and disappear.

When she gets to them, she ignores Carl completely and starts laying into Olly. I can't hear what she's saying, but you can see it's a telling-off. God knows what it's about. It goes on and on, and Olly just stares at her like she's mad, then she sticks her hand out and barks an order at him. I can see her saying the same thing three times. Eventually, he puts his packet of cigarettes in her hand. Without dropping her arm, she says something else, also three times, before he hands over his lighter. She puts the cigarettes and lighter into her handbag, then turns to Carl, says one thing, and strides away, with a cross but happy look on her face.

Both boys look from her to me and back again. They're not laughing. Not yet.

Before she reaches me, I spin on my heel and walk off, as fast as I can, away from all three of them. I don't run. I can't let Carl and Olly see me run.

Round the next corner, Mum catches up and tries to grab my arm.

'Come back,' she says.

'WHY DID YOU HAVE TO DO THAT?'

'Come here, Ben.'

'WHY DID YOU DO THAT?'

'Because I had to.'

'What did you say to them?'

'I just told him that, if he thinks I'm going to keep it from his mother that I've seen him smoking, he's got another think coming.'

Part of me is furious – that she's butted in and embarrassed me – but part of me is relieved that at least it wasn't about staying away from Carl or about her figuring out that Olly has betrayed me by being with him in secret. She's known Olly since he was three, so it could have been anything.

'And I told him what cigarettes will do to him. In no uncertain terms.'

Then she suddenly stops walking, and yanks me up close. She stares at me, eyeball to eyeball.

'Have you done this?' she says. 'Have you smoked?'

She's so fired up and mental she's almost making me forget that I want to kill her.

'No.'

'Promise me.'

'I haven't.'

'Promise me.'

'I haven't. I promise.'

'Good. Because I'd never forgive you.'

'Well, I'll never forgive *you*.' I'm trying to be angry again, but it doesn't really work. She's outdone me. 'He's my friend! It's none of your business.'

'I'm not joking, Ben,' she says. 'I'd be so disappointed in you. Whatever the other boys do, you don't have to join in. You've got to be yourself.'

She doesn't understand. She doesn't understand anything about what she's just done, and there's no way I can explain it to her. There's no point in even trying. Anyone who thinks you don't have to join in is too stupid to even talk to.

Even though she's staring right at me, waiting for me to speak, I don't open my mouth for ages, then I scowl at her and mutter, 'What did you say to Carl? At the end?'

'I just told him that what he did to Rachel was unforgivable. That he should be ashamed of himself.'

'What did he do to Rachel?' I want Mum's version. Donny's doesn't add up.

'That's none of your business.'

'What was it?'

'It's none of your business.'

'Tell me.'

She strides off.

After this, neither of us is in the mood to shop. We try for a bit, but it's all faked. We can't do it. It's probably the shortest trip to Brent Cross ever.

The red Mercedes is still there when we leave.

the bush in the playground

On the drive home, I don't say a word. I just stare out of the window, thinking. Mum stays quiet because she knows I'm cross.

My plan to win Olly back from Carl hasn't even got started. I should have known it wasn't going to work. There were plenty of signs. Clothes were the most obvious one. Only a couple of weeks into term, people had started talking about baggy trousers like they were an infectious disease. I always thought Olly didn't care about that kind of thing, but suddenly, without even mentioning it, his trousers all changed, and now he only wore drainpipes. The old ones never appeared again. He also chucked out his parka and changed to a leather jacket, which was a completely new thing for anyone to wear to school, but in a good way.

There was only one other boy I'd ever seen who had anything similar. I should have realized straight away, but I didn't notice until it was right in front of my eyes, at the Brent Cross fountains, the two of them, together, both in leather jackets.

There's no way in a million years I'll ever be allowed a leather jacket, but as we turn on to Kenton Road I decide that, as soon as we're home and Mum's put the kettle on, I'll make a bid for new trousers. She listens best when there's a cup of tea in her hand.

*

'We've just got back from the shops!' she says.

'I know,' I say. 'But I only just realized I need them.'

'We've been home two minutes! You decided in the last two minutes?'

'I was thinking about it in the car.'

'Unbelievable!' she says. 'Well, you'll have to wait. There's nothing wrong with what you've got, anyway.'

I try to tell her about drainpipes, but I'm too embarrassed to explain it properly – to say that I'm the last normal person not wearing them – and she tells me to grow up and stop making a fuss. 'Your trousers are almost new,' she says. 'You chose them yourself. At the end of the holidays.'

I can't say what I want to say, which is that everything's changed since then. I know it'll sound stupid.

'When you've outgrown them, you can have a new pair in whatever style you fancy,' she says, in a slow sing-song voice, like even she's making fun of me for behaving like a girl. I haven't explained that trousers are just the start. They're only the basic emergency, and there are other things I haven't even mentioned yet.

I end up using tricks I've learnt from Rachel, shouting and slamming doors and refusing to eat.

It's when I won't swallow any dinner that Mum finally takes me seriously, and with my plate sitting there between us, going cold, she agrees to a compromise. She says she'll take in the trousers on her sewing machine.

I make her do it right then, with me standing there in my pants, watching and eating. It's lucky she gives in because I'm starving and couldn't have held out much longer. Ten minutes, max. I don't know how Rachel does it. She can go days.

The trousers look a bit funny – they go out on the way to

the knees then in again down to the ankles – but it's at least an improvement and will get me off the hook at school (see fig. 9). It's maybe even the best outcome because it means I can look normal without Olly thinking I'm copying him.

FIGURE 9.

THE TROUSER SITUATION

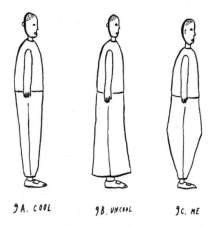

9A. COOL   9B. UNCOOL   9C. ME

I reckon that's the first time in my whole life I've worried I might be copying Olly.

Clothes were just one of the signs of him changing. The worst thing was that, even though he acted like my best friend in school, he'd started making excuses about the weekends. He kept saying he was busy, seeing cousins, or going on family trips, or running errands for his mum, and I believed him. Until Brent Cross, when I realized it was all lies.

So on the Monday after, I don't ring his bell. I go right past, for the first time ever, and walk all the way to school on my own. If Olly wants Carl, he can have him, but he can't have me as well.

I won't make a fuss about it, either. Moving desks is the best way to say I don't want to be Olly's friend any more, but it's too much. It'll make me look weak. I decide to just stop ringing him and stop visiting. At school, where I can't avoid him, I'll be normal. Cool, but normal. I won't argue, or accuse him of anything, or even tell him what I think. He'll just have to figure out that I've given up on him. And he'll never know I'm upset.

He gets in late, probably because he's been waiting for me, and Mrs Dickson gives him a telling-off that makes him go bright red. It's not very difficult to make Olly go red. The easiest way is to tell him he's blushing when he isn't, then he just does. On cue. It's funny every time.

Watching him getting told off, I realize that I hate him. The way things have changed is his fault. Carl's nasty, but he wouldn't be a problem if it wasn't for Olly. Olly's the one who's let everything go so wrong. He's the one who's betrayed me.

He's still red when he comes and sits next to me, and for the whole of maths we don't speak, but I can't tell if it's because of what's happened or just because he's already in trouble and doesn't want to get caught talking.

At playtime I walk off without saying anything. It's for him to try and get things back to normal, not me. Martin and Scott are picking teams when Olly comes over and says hi.

I say it back.

'Your mum rang my mum,' he says.

'Really?'

'Said what she saw.'

The way he says it, I almost say sorry. He's not acting cross, though. He's just telling me.

'You get in trouble?' I ask.

He nods.

'How badly?'

Then I get picked and have to go over to Martin's team. Olly ends up on the other side, and the game takes the whole of playtime, but at the end Olly comes over and stops me before we go into class.

'It wasn't your fault,' he says. 'I know it was her, not you.'

'OK,' I say.

'So we can just forget it happened,' he says.

What he's saying doesn't mean much, but the way he says it is a surprise. It feels as if this is his way of apologizing for lying to me. It's like he's asking to stay my friend.

He stands there, looking at me, waiting for me to speak, so I give him a big shove, pushing him into the bush that we always push each other into on the way to class.

He's not braced for it, so he goes right in, disappearing into the leaves. As soon as he's got his balance back, he dives out at me, but I'm already running away, laughing my head off. I let him catch up, and he drags me back, both of us grunting and yelping, and he takes his turn to shove me in, but it's not nearly as good as mine, then Mrs Dickson appears at the window, calls us 'horrible little vandals' and shouts at us to hurry up.

As we race up the stairs to the room, pulling each other back to make the other one last, I realize that perhaps in school things can stay the same. Perhaps we can still be friends.

Maybe I shouldn't accept it. Maybe I shouldn't let myself be relegated so easily. But that's not how you think. I'm too pleased he's being nice. I can't just throw it back at him.

olly's room

I have to test it out, though. I have to know what the weekend situation is. So, on Saturday, I call round. I don't ring up and see if he lies, or play any stupid games like that, I just go.

It's Olly's mum who answers the door. She's wearing a plungy top that makes her boobs look like two perfect scoops of ice cream. I reckon it would be really weird to have her as your mum. You wouldn't know where to look.

'Go on up,' she says.

I give her my best smile as I climb the stairs. It freezes on my face when I walk into Olly's bedroom and find Carl sitting there on the carpet. Olly's opposite him. They're in the middle of a game of cards.

Olly goes red straight away, and doesn't even say hello. Carl just grins, like he's pleased to see me, but in a scary way – in the way a dog would be pleased to see a steak.

'All right?' I say.

Carl nods. No one says anything. We just stare at each other, the silence getting longer and longer.

'What are you playing?' I say, eventually. It's the only thing I can think of.

'Nothing,' says Carl.

He's lying. You can see from the way the cards are laid out that they're in the middle of something. They've got a hand each, and the pack's between them, mostly face down, with a smaller, messier pile face up.

'Is it rummy?' I say.

Carl shakes his head and dumps the cards he's holding on to the floor. He takes Olly's, too, puts all the cards together and starts shuffling them. 'We were just going to play knuckles. D'you know knuckles?'

I shrug a yes, even though I don't. Carl stands and walks towards me.

'It's supposed to be two players, but you can play with three,' he says, and holds the pack out to me, flat in the palm of his hand, so you can tell he's not passing it over, but wants me to cut.

I do it and get the nine of hearts.

'What's the rules?' I say.

'I thought you knew,' says Carl.

'They might be different from yours,' I say.

'So you tell me what you think, and I'll say if it's the same.'

He's almost got me, but not quite. 'Mine doesn't start with a cut, so it's already different. We might as well play yours.'

'How does yours start?'

'JUST TELL US THE RULES, YOU IDIOT!'

He smiles, like he's already winning. 'Everyone cuts,' he says. 'The winner has the highest card. Loser the lowest. Picture cards are ten. Ace is eleven. The loser holds out his fist. The winner hits the loser on the knuckles with the pack of cards, as many times as the value of the winning card. The winner's the one who bottles out last. The loser's whoever bottles out first. And you can't bottle out in the middle of a round.'

I look at Olly. Olly looks at me.

'That's not a card game,' I say.

'What is it, ballet?' he says. 'You've got a nine.'

He holds the pack out to Olly. Olly hesitates. 'What if it's a draw?'

'You have a play-off,' he says. 'You recut. Come on.'

Carl jabs Olly in the belly with the pack of cards. Olly cuts.

'Four!' says Carl. 'Bad luck.'

Holding the pack up high, Carl theatrically lowers his hand on to the thin pile of cards and pauses for effect, looking from me to Olly. With a flourish, he cuts, and sweeps his card round in front of our eyes before looking at it himself.

'Oooooooooooooh! Eight!' he says. 'You win.'

Carl and Olly both hand me their cards, and I shuffle them all together into a pack. I don't really know what to do.

'Come on. Hand out,' says Carl.

Olly does as he's told.

'In a fist. In a fist,' says Carl.

Olly forms a fist, fingers down, and points it towards me.

'Go on, then,' says Carl. 'Nine.'

I grip the pack, not too hard, but not so loosely that I might drop any, and bring it down on the back of Olly's hand.

'One,' says Carl.

Carl counts them all off. I don't hit too hard, but at the end of it Olly's first two knuckles are red and a bit puffy. By the last few hits, I'm quite enjoying it.

As the winner, it's me to offer the pack for the next round. Olly gets six, Carl a Queen, then me a nine.

'Unlucky again!' says Carl, so excited he's almost singing it. He grabs the cards off me, positions Olly's fist where he wants it, and gives him ten, about the same hardness as I did. He angles the pack slightly to get different knuckles to the ones I got. By the end, Olly's skin isn't broken, but you can see it's sore.

Next round, I draw first and get an ace. I can't help dancing round the room and gloating because I know I'm safe straight away.

Olly's next and gets a king, which sets me off dancing again. It's so perfect. It's going to be me on Carl, with eleven hits.

'It's a king!' I shout. 'It's a king!'

Carl, cutting as flashily as ever, gets a three. Extra humiliation.

'THREE! Come on, Carl! You've got to do better than that!' I say.

He hands over his cards and holds out his fist straight away, not looking down at it like Olly, but staring straight into my eyes, like he's daring me. It's a brilliant moment. I take my time over getting the pack in order, and do to Carl what he did to Olly, positioning the fist exactly where I want it to get a good swing at him.

The sound of the first hit is completely different. I'm doing it about twice as hard as on Olly. The first one brings up a little blip of skin, like a tiny blister, on Carl's middle knuckle. Carl doesn't even look down at it. He just eyeballs me, blinking slowly like he's never been calmer.

'One,' he says, in a tone of voice that sounds like he's saying one–nil to him.

My second one's a bit harder, aimed at the same knuckle, but I don't get as good a connection.

'Two,' says Carl, still with a slightly gloaty ring.

By number eight, there's a proper flap of skin that's lifted up, and you can see red underneath. By ten, it's not just redness, but proper blood. With the last hit, I even get a little smudge on the bottom card. I show it to Carl.

'Well done,' he says, in a way that's doubly sarcastic because he doesn't say it sarcastically, but as if he means it.

My heart's beating fast now. I've got that total focus and concentration which blots out everything in the world except the game you're playing. I know I'm going to win. I really feel it's my day.

I hold out the pack.

Olly – five of clubs.

Carl – eight of diamonds.

This is so easy. I'm not even scared.

I do a Carl-style cut, lifting up and out so the others see my card before I do. I can't believe it when I flip my hand over and see the two of spades. A two! With only eight to beat!

'Unlucky,' says Carl, quietly. Not gloating.

Carl gathers the cards and positions my fist where he wants it. While he's doing this, I notice his grip on the pack. He's not holding it flat, but vertically, the way you'd hold a knife if you were going to stab it down into a table. As he gets ready, I can see he's going to hit down on me like that, with the edge of the pack, not with the flat of it, like before.

'You can't do it like that,' I say.

'Why not?'

'You just can't.'

'There's no rule about how you hold the pack.'

'That's not how we've been playing.'

'I can do it how I want.'

'It's not fair.'

'It's not cheating.'

'I'm not playing if you're going to do it differently.'

'Can't bottle out in the middle of a round.'

'You can't change the rules in the middle of a round.'

'I'm not changing the rules. You're the one that's trying to change the rules by bottling out.'

'I'm not bottling out.'

'Good. So hold out your hand.'

'Not if you're going to hit like that.'

'Olly?' says Carl. 'Was there anything about how you hold the pack in the rules?'

Olly looks from Carl to me to Carl again. He shakes his head.

'And he can't bottle in the middle of a round, can he?'

Olly doesn't look at me this time. He doesn't even really look at Carl. He just shrugs.

'There you go, then,' says Carl, putting my fist where he wants it.

I'm still trying to think of an answer when the first hit gets me. It's so hard that my hand is knocked right down to my side. The corner of the pack has dug right in behind my biggest knuckle, and a curl of skin has flipped upwards. Underneath, there's colourless stuff that isn't skin. It's whitish, then it goes red in front of my eyes. I feel like someone's stuck a big needle into me and left it there.

'One,' says Carl.

My heart's thumping and my brain's racing, but it also feels as if nothing's happening up there. It's like my head's gone numb. It's like I can't stop what Carl's doing. He repositions my fist where he wants it and raises the pack not up to shoulder height like before, but right above his head, as far up as it'll go. He hits again. This one's even harder and it's on exactly the same spot. You'd think he was trying to bang in a nail.

'Two,' he says.

It feels more like a knife than a pack of cards. The pain shoots up my arm as if everything's screeching inside. A bead of blood comes out of the hole in my skin, a perfect little, red blob that with Carl's third hit splodges all over the knuckle.

116

He counts them off, right up to eight, his tone of voice trying to stay the same, but gradually changing as he stops being able to hide how much he's enjoying himself. His cheeks, which are normally so pale you can almost see through them, become flushed with colour as if he's eaten a big bowl of hot soup.

By the time he finishes, my eyes are pricking with tears and my whole body feels trembly, but when I look down at myself, everything's still.

My hand's a mess. Sometimes you forget it's you all the way to the middle of your body, in different layers of red squelchiness. My knuckles look like someone's ripped me open to see what's inside – to see if it's still me under the surface.

It's when I see Olly staring that it's hardest not to cry. You'd think my hand was dead by the way Olly gawps at it, with his mouth wide open, eyes not blinking.

My chest's going up and down like I've been running. I can only get air into me in gasps. I try to breathe normally, but I can't. Through a blur of tears, I look up and see Carl's hand stretched out flat, the cards neatly piled in his palm. It's my turn to cut.

I've got to the end of the round. I haven't cried. I haven't bottled out. If I leave now, it's OK. I've lost, but I haven't been humiliated. If I take a card, I'm in for the round, and I could lose again. I could easily lose again to Carl. But if I don't take a card, I've missed the opportunity to get him back.

Chances are, it'll be my turn on him, now he's had his turn on me. I can easily hit just as hard as him. I can show him what it feels like. He's cheated by hitting me with the edge of the pack, and he should pay for it. It's not fair if he doesn't have it done back to him.

For ages I stare at the cards. No one says anything or tries to rush me. They know what I'm thinking. The edge of the pack is splodged with red. No one'll be able to use it again without thinking of my split-open hand.

Sometimes when you're deciding what to do, you act like you're thinking about the different options, but you're not really thinking anything. You're just waiting to see what your body does. It's as if your body tells your head what to do, not the other way round. You're just waiting, not thinking.

It's a surprise when it happens – when my arm goes out and picks a card. The real shock is when I look at it. It's the four of clubs.

Olly's next. Ten of diamonds.

Then Carl. We see the card before he does. Queen of hearts.

'Unlucky, Ben. It's me and you again,' he says.

'No. It's ten all. It's a play-off.'

'Queen's higher than a ten.'

'Not according to your rules,' I say. 'Ten's ten and queen's ten. That's a draw.'

'But a queen's higher. I won.'

'It's not higher. It's a ten.'

'Queen always beats ten.'

'Not if a queen is a ten. It's a draw. They're your rules. It's a play-off. You and Olly.'

Carl shrugs, like he can't be bothered to waste his time talking to me and holds what's left of the pack out to Olly. Olly cuts again. Jack. Then Carl. Five.

It's Olly on me. I could run for it now and they wouldn't stop me, but it'd look bad, and I'd miss out on my chance to get Carl back. Olly won't hit me any harder than I hit him. With my hand the way it is, though, anything is going to really hurt.

I hold my fist out, and Olly stares at it as he gathers the pack together.

'You can submit now if you like,' says Olly.

'No, he can't,' Carl butts in.

I shake my head. 'Don't want to,' I say.

Olly takes my hand and positions it in the best spot. He holds it gently, and I can feel the warmth of his fingers against mine, which are cold and shaky. In his other hand he's got the pack of cards. He's not holding it stabbing fashion, like Carl, but normally, like before.

He raises the pack towards my red and pulpy knuckles, and holds it still, measuring the distance for his hit. I can see that the pack is trembling in his hand. He's breathing fast and noisily through his nose. For ages, he doesn't move.

'You can't even do it!' says Carl. 'You're such a dork!'

Then the pack goes up and bangs down into my knuckles.

After such a long wait, it comes when I'm not expecting it, and I can't stop myself crying out in pain. Even though he's not doing it nearly as hard as Carl, it's just as sore. My hand went slightly numb first time round, but now I can feel everything.

'One,' says Carl.

Olly positions himself for a second hit, and there's another long pause. Finally, it comes. I'm more prepared this time, and I don't make any noise, but a tear that's been building up in one eye spills over and runs down my cheek. I try and wipe it away before the other two notice, but they both see.

'Two,' says Carl.

Olly puts the cards out again, ready for his third hit, and this time the wait goes on and on. Eventually he says, 'I resign. I've lost.'

'Don't be a girl,' says Carl.

'I'll be what I want. I've lost,' says Olly. 'I don't care.'

'You can't resign in the middle of a round.'

'I don't want to play any more,' he says.

He drops the cards on the floor, walks away and lies on the bed, staring up at the ceiling. You can see that nothing's going to change his mind.

Carl scoops up the cards, shuffles them into a pack and holds them out to me, his clear blue eyes glinting with how much fun he's having.

'Me v. you for winner, then,' he says.

I stare down at the pack, stacked neatly on Carl's palm. If I lost again, I reckon he could cut through to the bone.

'Did you learn this at the unit?' I say. 'From the other psychos?'

He shrugs. 'Your cut,' he says.

I slap the underside of his hand and cards fly everywhere.

'I'm bored,' I say. 'I'm going home.'

And I walk out.

On the way back, I rub some gravel from the driveway of number 30 into my cheek, so I can tell Mum I fell off my bike. Before she sees them, I put plasters on my knuckles.

She believes the story, but at dinner I can tell by the way Donny looks at me that he knows I've lied.

On Monday, Olly stares at my hand right through register, and on the way to assembly he tries to apologize for what happened.

'He's not normally like that,' he says. 'I reckon he's just got it in for you.'

'I'm going to move desks,' I say.

There's a spare place near the door, sharing with Eric, who only ever gets called Blob. It's like Siberia back there, but I have to do it.

Blob's only friend is Kwok, who's new and doesn't speak English. Kwok's got a brother in the year below who also can't speak English, and who's also called Kwok. They're both tiny. Three Kwoks would weigh one Blob.

the view from next to blob

I need special permission from Mrs Dickson to move, and she warns me that I won't be allowed to go back. You can't change desks more than once a term. I don't even hesitate. I just tell her I have to do it.

At the back, next to Blob, it's another world. All I'm thinking about when I ask to move is who I'm getting away from. It doesn't cross my mind to worry who I'm going towards. It's a long time since Blob had anyone sitting next to him and, as far as he's concerned, I'm his saviour. I'm his new friend. Fact is, I'd rather saw my own legs off than be Blob's friend. If you're willing to be seen with him, you might as well give up. You can't sink any lower than Blob.

But when you're sitting next to him, he's not so easy to avoid. I can't tell him to go away and shut up, which is what I want to do every time he tries to talk to me, because we're stuck at the same desk. Normally, you just avoid Blob. Everyone does. But now I can't.

Every day, as soon as I sit down, he starts right in asking me what I did last night and what I watched on telly and what I had for dinner, coming out with stupid question after stupid question. He doesn't have a clue about how normal people talk, and it just goes on and on. You can see how happy he is that he's got someone to talk to, even when I hardly answer him. I never ask him anything back, and he doesn't even mind.

None of the normal ways of letting someone know you don't like them work on Blob. He's always too close and too loud and too keen, and there's nothing I can do to make him leave me alone. It's being seen talking to him that I hate, but I can't avoid it.

One day he turns up at school carrying a thin pile of envelopes. I reckon there's only about four of them and, when he gives me one, I have a horrible feeling about what it's going to be. No one's watching, so I open it as quick as I can, in front of him, and it's exactly what I was afraid of. It's an invitation to his birthday party.

He stands there, gazing at me with his big, wet eyes, waiting for an answer. It's the best opportunity I've had to shake him off. I'd never go to his party in a million years, and if I just say that to him – if I just tell him the truth – then he'll have to stop pestering me. All it would take is to say no. It wouldn't be so cruel. I'd be doing him a favour.

But I just mumble, 'Thanks,' and slip the invitation into my desk.

It's register, except Mrs Dickson hasn't arrived yet, so everyone's mucking about. Most of the boys are running round after Martin, who's got a ball he won't throw to anyone except Scott, and the girls are in gossipy little groups, mainly near Verity's desk. Olly isn't there yet, even though it's late. A few days recently he hasn't turned up at all and, even though he brings a note, I think he's bunking. His mum's got a typewriter.

I watch Blob go round the room. He gives the next envelope to Kwok, who smiles and nods, and puts it in his desk. Blob mimes that he wants Kwok to open it in front of him, but Kwok doesn't understand and just keeps smiling and nodding, until Blob gives up.

He goes over to James next, who's a bit blotchy and smells of wee. James sits next to Kwok on the desk in front of us. James takes the envelope and says in a voice so loud that everyone stops and stares, 'EEEERRRRR – WHAT'S THIS?'

Blob tenses up. Everyone's looking at him, even Martin and Scott. 'It's an invitation,' he says, so quietly you can hardly hear him.

'TO WHAT?'

Blob takes ages to answer, and eventually just tries to snatch the envelope back, but James is too quick and he pulls it out of reach, then stands on a chair so Blob can't reach him.

With everyone watching, James opens the envelope and reads aloud at the top of his voice: 'PLEASE COME TO MY PARTY ON SUNDAY 3RD. 8 GLENWOOD CLOSE. 3 TILL 6. GAMES! CLOWNS! TRAMPOLINING!'

'*CLOWNS?*' says Scott.

'How are you going to do trampolining?' says Martin. 'You won't bounce – you'll just blob.'

Everyone laughs, even the girls.

'CAN I COME? CAN I COME?' shouts Scott.

'You can have mine,' says James and chucks him the invitation.

It's not a good throw, and Blob runs after it, but Scott gets there first. He chucks it to Martin, and like an idiot Blob runs round and round the room trying to get it back, until Mrs Dickson comes in and tells him off. While she's shouting at him, Martin deliberately stands where Blob can see and rips the invitation up into tiny pieces, which he sprinkles on Blob's chair.

People are horrible to Blob because they're afraid of him. They aren't scared he can hurt you or do anything bad to you; they're afraid in the way you'd be afraid of a disease. The outcast disease. If you get too close, you might catch it. And I'm too close.

I'd never have thought it was possible. I've always had lots of friends. People like me. But from the back of the class, next to Blob, I begin to feel that everything's slipping away. The minute I don't have Olly, I don't seem to have anyone.

However nasty I am to Blob, however much I try to show everyone that I'm not his friend, I can feel people are beginning to think of me differently, and the harder I try to get things back to normal, the worse they become.

I start getting picked later and later for football at playtime, and when Blob comes and asks if he can join in, which he never normally does, I can tell it's because I'm there – because he thinks I might let him play. Usually I wouldn't mind. I wouldn't want him on my team, but I wouldn't mind him playing. Now, though, it makes me so crazy that he thinks he's my friend, and that he lets himself show it in front of other people, that I just start swearing at him and telling him he's too fat for football, and then I'm kicking him, again and again, on his big, flabby bum, and he starts crying, but I still don't stop.

When I turn round, I think everyone's going to be laughing, but they're not. They're just looking at me like I'm nuts, and I realize I've made everything worse.

The day after that, Blob tells me his party's cancelled.

I always thought you were where you were. I thought things stayed put. Now I know different. The world's slippery. All it takes is for one thing to shift, and everything can slide away. People you've known for years can change their mind about you just like that, without warning, not one at a time, but all at once, in a gang. As soon as you touch the outcasts, you become one of them, and everyone just abandons you. It's like falling off the edge of the world.

Even Mum notices, and starts asking me why I'm acting funny and not going out, and why I don't see Olly any more.

'Is it because he smokes?' she asks.

'I DO STILL SEE HIM,' I say. 'I SEE HIM AT SCHOOL EVERY DAY. HE'S MY BEST FRIEND.' I don't know why I'm shouting.

'Why don't you see him at the weekends? Have you fallen out?'

'NO!'

She frowns and asks me what's wrong, so I leave the kitchen and slam the door.

She follows me all the way up to my room, sits on the edge of the bed, and starts saying in a slow, quiet voice, like she's explaining a chemical formula and we're the only two scientists in the world who understand it, that she doesn't want me spending time with boys who smoke, and she'll be livid if she ever suspects me of smoking, but she doesn't want me to think I shouldn't go out at all. 'The world's full of people who do bad things, and everyone does some bad things,' she says, 'but that doesn't mean you should hide yourself away from everyone. Just because I got cross with him doesn't mean you should never see him again. The last thing I want is you just moping around at home. He's your best friend. You should visit him. And if you don't want to see him, you should start seeing other people. You can't just stay in all the time. Just because Rachel's doing it doesn't mean it's grown-up or clever. You have to go out and do things.'

She's so way off and so stupid I want to cry. I can feel tears coming, but not because I'm upset. It's just anger and frustration and the way no one understands what's happening, so I run off again, this time out of the house and down the street. I don't have anywhere to go, so I just wander round, thinking, trying to figure out what I can do to make things better, but I don't have a single idea. I can't think of anything that could get my life back to how it was. I can't think of how I'll ever be normal and have normal friends ever again.

Mum wanting things to be better just makes everything worse. The way she stares at me, like she's always trying to figure out why I'm not happy, makes me crosser and crosser, and makes me want to tell her less and less, and just seeing that look in her eyes reminds me straight away about everything that's wrong, and everything I least want to think about.

I hate her. I hate Mum and I hate everyone else, too.

mcdonald's

For Olly, things change just as fast. All his life he's had me to keep him on track, but now I won't even speak to him. He tries with me for a while, but when he realizes I'm not just in a temporary huff he gives up, and soon we both act as if the other one's invisible.

Carl's got him now. It's game over. He's beaten me.

Which means Carl has to think of a new game, and by watching how Olly changes I can guess what it is. I don't know what the rules are, or how it's going to happen, but I know for certain that it's about winning and losing, and that Olly's going to lose.

Without me sitting next to him, straight away Olly's attention begins to wander in class. He starts getting in trouble for not listening, and then for not doing his work. He chucks things around with Scott and Martin, but it's never them that get caught, it's always Olly.

Some boys enjoy being in trouble, but you can tell Olly hates it. You can tell he doesn't ever quite know what's going to happen next. He's got a different look in his eyes now, sleepier and more alert at the same time, like he can't be bothered to do much, but is ready every second to defend himself. And I'm sure he's bunking. I don't know where he goes, or what he does, but it's easy enough to guess who he's with.

On days when he bunks, I sit there at the back, listening to Blob's snorty, wheezy breathing, staring at what's rightfully my desk, with two empty seats tucked under it, and I get so angry I just want to stand up and smash everything. But I don't even know who to blame. I can't decide who I hate most.

a) Olly
b) Carl
c) Myself
d) Mum
e) Blob
f) The boys who bully Blob, and could any day turn on me

It's multiple choice. Circle the correct letter.

Usually multiple choice is easy, but I don't know the answer to this one unless it's one big oval round all the letters. Everything I used to enjoy has been taken away. And as I stare at those two empty seats, picking at the scabs on my knuckles, I realize I have to do something to save myself. I have to take drastic action to stop my slide towards the living death of becoming like Blob.

There's only one option. I have to get back in with Olly and Carl.

It's Thursdays when Olly bunks most. Don't know why, it just is, so the next Thursday I head off for school, like normal, but don't go any further than Olly's house. I hover near the corner where I can see his door but he can't see me.

He comes out at the usual time and heads off in the direction of school. I watch him go left at the bottom of the street – the normal route – and I follow him at a safe distance, doing the same sprinting and hiding thing as when me and Olly tailed Carl back to his house. It's odd, remembering that now. It feels as if we were different people back then, but it's only a few weeks ago.

At the bottom of Hawthorne Avenue, he does just what I'm expecting. He doesn't go straight on, down Francis Road towards school, but cuts left on to the back roads that come out near the cinema.

My heart's beating fast as I follow, and I get so engrossed in the excitement of following him I almost forget that, for the first time in my life, I'm bunking school. It's only when I see a boy with schoolbags and PE kit coming the other way that I remember what I'm doing. He gives me a suspicious look as he walks past because it's obvious I'm up to something, but I pull a face back and he runs off. He's only a little one, and he won't know my name.

Olly's easy to follow in a crowd because of that hair. The closer we get to the town centre, the more people there are, and the easier it is to stay hidden. He goes right at the Granada, and straight on, past Debenhams, up to the town centre. At Sally, the skipping girl, he looks at his watch and just stands there for a bit, as if he's early for something. I press myself back into the entranceway of Boots, and he doesn't see me.

I'm guessing he's going to go right, to the shopping centre, but he doesn't. After hovering around the statue for a bit, looking up a couple of times at where Sally's knickers ought to be, he goes straight on, up Station Road. I used to always get Station Road and St Ann's Road mixed up, until Dad told me Station Road was the one with the station on it. Now it's easy.

Outside McDonald's he checks his watch again, and goes in.

For ages, I can't make myself go any further. Just the idea of walking up to them and waiting to see how they react makes my throat go dry. I don't even know what I'll say. I can imagine myself saying hi, but can't think of what should come next. I can't think of how to act. Then I realize that, if Olly's early,

Carl could just turn up at any minute and see me standing there like an idiot. Even worse, he could come up behind and catch me by surprise.

I take off round the corner and press myself against the wall of Ryman's. I can't let either of them spot me in a moment of indecision. The whole thing has to look completely casual. My heart's pounding as I stand there, and my knees feel almost too weak to hold me up. Part of me just wants to run for it, back to school, or back home. I could pretend to be ill. I've got all the symptoms. Just standing there not knowing what to do next is like having flu, like the whole world's pressing in on your head so hard that everything goes fuzzy and you just want to lie down and sleep.

A while later I see Carl go past at the bottom of the street, walking with his usual strut, hands in his pockets, on the way to McDonald's.

The longer I leave it, the more questions they'll ask, and the longer they'll realize I was following them, which will just make me look weirder. I have to get going. It's the scariest thing I've ever done. Scarier than cycling to Wembley, scarier than chicken on the railway tracks, scarier than knuckles against Carl, but I have to do it. I've run out of choices. I have to go in.

My hand's shaking as it pushes open the doors, and I'm out of breath. Inside, there's the usual comforting smell – like chips, sweets, bleach and sick all mixed up in a bucket – and I've got a while to get ready for them because all the tables are upstairs. Now I'm in there, I realize I'm going to have to buy something. I've only got 50p, so I order small fries, which is the cheapest thing after a ketchup cup, and I don't reckon they let you sit down if all you order is ketchup cups.

With my one portion of small fries on a tray, and my

schoolbag hanging heavily on my shoulder, I trudge up the stairs. It's like walking to the headmaster's office.

Before I turn the corner to face the room, I arrange my face into the most relaxed shape I can manage, as if I'm so relaxed I'm bored.

They're right in the furthest corner of the restaurant, slunk down in their seats, each sipping a drink, probably a Coke or a milkshake. I wish that's what I'd ordered now, but it's too late to turn round, and I don't have the money anyway. I see them before they see me, which is good, and I walk straight towards them, as confidently as I can, looking in their direction, but not catching anyone's eye. I plonk my tray on their table and sit down.

First I eat a couple of chips, then I say, 'All right?'

I look at Olly first. He shrugs, his face blank. I look across at Carl. You can't tell what he's thinking. Then, without any warning, he smiles. A big, beaming smile.

'Chips!' he says. 'Just what the doctor ordered!' And he takes a big handful. A small fries isn't really much more than one handful, but I don't mind. It seems like a good start.

'You often have chips for breakfast, then?' he asks.

'Sometimes,' I say. It's a total lie. Mum would kill me if she saw me in Maccy D's for breakfast. 'You often have milkshake?' I say. You can tell by the shadow of it staying up in the straw that it's not Coke.

'Sometimes,' he says.

There's a silence while I finish my chips and Olly polishes off his drink. Olly doesn't even want to look at me until he knows where things stand. I can sense how nervous he is from the way he's gurgling the milkshake. I try not to look up much, either, and just concentrate on my chips as if they're the only interesting thing in the room. I eat what's left of them as slowly as I can.

'Why aren't you at school, then?' says Carl, eventually.

I shrug. 'Couldn't be bothered,' I say. 'Why aren't *you* at school?' I deliberately say 'school', not 'the unit'.

He thinks for a while before shrugging, and saying with a smirk, 'Couldn't be bothered.'

When he says that, I know things are probably OK. I've played it by his rules, but I haven't been too desperate or sucky, and I reckon it's worked. The relief of it feels like a knot untangling in my belly.

For the first time, it occurs to me that maybe Carl wanted me back all along. It stands to reason, really. If you're going to be in charge, being in charge of two is twice as good as being in charge of one. And if Olly's the only person in your gang, it's not really much of a gang. Carl's definitely better off with me than without me. All he wanted was to make sure he was the boss.

It isn't going to be so bad, not being in charge. Compared to having no one, it's hardly bad at all.

'How d'you find us?' he says, but not in a nasty way. It sounds more like he's impressed.

'Just a guess,' I say.

He seems to believe it. Sounds better than saying I followed.

'What d'you want to do today?' he asks, looking at me with all the spooky blueness of his eyes.

I shrug.

'We're going nicking,' he says. 'Wanna come?'

From the way Olly's head jerks up, I can tell this is news to him. The plan must have changed because of me. I don't know why Olly's surprised. It's obvious Carl would make me do something more than just bunking. I have to show I've crossed over to his side. He needs more proof that I'm really in.

Either that, or it's a trap. It's possible he'd set me up to get caught as one last victory. Maybe he won't be happy until I'm chucked out of school altogether and sent to a unit, just like him. Maybe that's how he wants to finally beat me.

I shrug at him, not exactly a yes, not exactly a no. I've never stolen anything in my life, and I can't say I'm keen.

'What d'you want to nick?' he says.

the sweet shop

Three kids in a sweet shop in the middle of the day, we stand out a mile. From the first minute we're in there, the guy behind the counter starts shouting, 'One at a time! One at a time!'

There's a sign on the door saying no more than two school-children at once, but he's obviously taken against us and lowered the number.

'It says two outside!' Carl says.

'Only one!'

'So why'd's it say two?'

'Get out, please. Just one.'

'You can't just change the rules like that. It's prejudice.'

'I can do what I like. It's my shop. Get out. All of you.'

'All of us? You said one a minute ago!'

'Well, now it's zero. I don't like your attitude.'

'What have I done?'

'I'll give you five seconds.'

'I've got rights. I've got human rights.'

The newsagent lifts up the counter flap and ducks under it to come and chuck us out. During the moment when his head's under the counter, I grab a packet of Polos and slip them into my coat pocket. It feels sneaky and low and dirty, and as my hand reaches out I sense that I'm losing something I can never get back, but I know I have to get it over with. Until I've shown I can nick, we'll be going from shop to shop, and the longer we spin it out, the more chance there is of getting caught. It's better to do it when Carl's distracted, too, since that covers me against a set-up.

'You said I had five seconds!' says Carl. 'I want to buy something.'

'Too late.'

'That wasn't five seconds!'

He grabs Carl by the arm and starts shoving him out. Carl wriggles, but doesn't really fight him off. 'You should be in school,' says the newsagent, as he's trying to squeeze Carl through the door.

'I only wanted to buy some fags,' Carl says.

'Well, I don't sell them to children.'

'What if I go to the pigs and tell them you do?'

'What if I smash your head open on the pavement?'

As he says it, the newsagent gives Carl a massive push into the street, then turns back to me and Olly. We're standing right next to him, waiting by the door, so he doesn't need to touch us. We shuffle out without even being told. The Polos in my pocket feel radioactive as I go past, and for a moment I'm sure the man's going to sense what I've got and grab me.

Then I'm outside. Safe. Carl starts shouting to him through the door, saying 'One at a time! One at a time!' over and over again, making fun of the newsagent's Indian accent, twanging the Ts like rubber bands. Olly starts laughing and joining in, so even though it isn't funny I have to join in, too.

I'm glad when Carl gives up and we get to walk off. When we're round the corner I tell them I did it.

'Did what?' says Carl.

'Nicked,' I say. 'Nicked something.'

'When?' he says.

'Just now. When he was ducking under the counter I grabbed some stuff.'

'Hey! Super slicko!' says Carl, like he's really impressed. 'Such a pro!'

'It was easy,' I say, trying not to smile or look too pleased.

'Show us, then,' he says. 'Show us the stash.'

I get out the Polos.

'And?' he says.

'That's it.'

'That's it? *Polos!*'

'Yeah.'

'That's all you got?'

'Yeah.'

'Polos?'

'Yeah.'

'*Polos?*'

'What's wrong with Polos?'

'Who eats Polos, you div?'

'Everyone.' I say.

'No, they don't.'

He grabs them out of my hand and chucks the full, unopened packet into the street. They skid all the way out to the middle, then roll back on the slope of the tarmac, squeezing between the wheels of a couple of cars, before getting squidged flat by a lorry.

'Why didn't you get chocolate, you idiot?'

'Dunno.'

'You've got a whole shop of anything you want, and you get *Polos?*'

I shrug.

'You'll have to nick something else,' he says.

★

We end up in Smiths. I swipe a pen and a bottle of Tippex. Olly almost gets some tapes, but chickens out at the last minute, probably because he can't choose between D90, AD90 and AR90. Carl's not very impressed with my haul, and makes me write 'BEN SMELLS' on a bench with the Tippex, but after that he stops telling me I have to nick more stuff, and I seem to be in the clear.

It's a weird day, but probably less difficult than I expected. And at the end of it, I'm pretty sure I've turned things round. I'm back in.

the grass behind the busted water fountain

After that, things get back to normal. Not old normal, but a new normal. I bunk off about once a week, and the three of us spend weekends together, mostly hanging around the shopping centre or mucking about in the park.

When we bunk, we often go to the racetrack, where we used to play on our bikes. It's a risky place to be because you can see our school from there. They'd need binoculars to see you, but it still feels chancy. Only someone like Carl would think of bunking right under their noses.

It's when we're there one Thursday that Carl offers me my first cigarette. I say no, but Carl just keeps holding the packet out to me, not moving a muscle, and that's how I know it's an order, not an offer.

I put the cigarette in my mouth, and Olly strikes a match, so I take it from my lips and hold it in the flame.

'Has to be in your mouth, you idiot,' says Olly.

I try that and it still won't light. The paper round the end's getting browner and browner.

'Suck. Suck it,' he says.

The match has burnt up to his fingers now, so he shakes it and drops it. That's when I notice there are loads of cigarette butts and burnt matches around our feet, which are probably theirs. He lights another one and holds it out. This time I suck, and the flame leans towards me, as if by magic. Straight away my mouth fills with the worst fumes I've ever tasted. It's like all the dust under your bed multiplied by car exhaust multiplied by farts and beetroot. It's like putting your head in a hoover bag and taking a deep breath. It's the most disgusting thing *ever*, and even though I know you have to not cough, it's about a hundredth of a second before I'm bent double, choking my lungs out.

You'd think Carl would be laughing, but he isn't. He just watches, with a little half-smile on his face. By the way he looks at me when I stop coughing, I know I have to keep going until I've finished the cigarette.

I look across at Olly, and he gives me a tiny look of encouragement, but he doesn't say anything. I check it's still alight, and unfortunately it is, with a thin string of smoke snaking up from the tip.

I suck gently this time, and it doesn't make me cough quite so much. If I concentrate, I can get most of the smoke out of my mouth before it leaks down my throat. It still hurts, though. Every puff feels like someone's scraping the inside of my neck with a washing-up brush.

I'm only halfway through when my head suddenly feels weightless and empty, like my brain's disappeared, and I realize I'm going to fall over. When cartoon characters bang their heads, you hear tweeting noises and little stars go round and round their heads. I've never known why, but I've never wondered, either. Now, just as I feel like I'm going to topple over, I start seeing little sparkles of white light in the top of my vision, dancing around, just like the stars in cartoons, and I realize that's what it must mean. If your head goes funny enough, you really do see stars. The difference is, only you see them. In cartoons everyone sees them. There's no tweeting, though. The tweeting's made up.

Just before my legs give way, I stagger for the fence and grab hold of it. Everything begins to go dark, closing in from the edges of my eyes like the end of an old film, then it gets light again, and my head feels like it might be returning to normal. But suddenly there's a jolt inside me, and I'm bent over, puking. It comes out in a big splash that gets my shoes and the bottom of my trousers.

My stomach squelches and lurches, again and again, even when there's nothing more to come up. By the time I can stand straight again, my throat feels scrubbed raw, and my tummy's a cold pebble inside me.

When you finish puking, it's like coming out of a dream. It's a slight surprise to find I'm still in the park, and I've almost forgotten Carl and Olly are there.

'You OK?' says Olly, eventually.

I nod, and spit. It's hard to get any saliva. I glance at Carl, but he won't look at me. He's looking at the sick. I follow his eyes, and my heart starts hammering when I see what he's staring at.

My cigarette's right there, in the middle of it, half smoked. From the look in Carl's eyes, I feel sure he's going to make me pick it out and finish it. Even if it won't light, he'll make me try.

If he does, I don't know what I'll do. I don't know if I'll be able to stop myself grabbing him and shoving his face into the sick, grinding it as hard as I can until he's breathing it in and choking on it. I'll press his nose into the ground till it bleeds, so his blood mixes with my puke and he has to swallow both. I won't care what he does back to me. I won't even care.

It's ages before he speaks. Finally, he lifts his gaze from the vomit and stares right into my eyes. The way he looks at me these days, I feel like he knows what I'm thinking. He probably doesn't, or he'd kick me out, but the idea that he might – the idea that he could know how much I hate him – is petrifying.

'That stinks,' he says. 'Let's go.'

I sit next to Olly in class again now, with special permission from Mrs Dickson, but we don't always walk in together. Sometimes I call for him, often I don't.

When it's just the two of us, without Carl, things are a bit strange. We can't quite keep up all the attitude, but we can't let it drop either, or we'd look like frauds. You don't want it to seem like the whole thing's just a mask you can take off at will.

I'm no different at home. I'm just the same as always. I reckon Olly is, too, so we probably could be normal with each other, but it never happens.

Once it almost does. We're walking back from school, and we've both stamped on Coke cans, which we're wearing clamped on to our shoes like big, clompy heels. We're clattering around, making noises with our feet, and I start trying to kick his cans off, so he goes for mine, and we have a bit of a scrap, which makes a huge racket with all the clanking and scraping of the metal against the path, and we both ended up on top of each other on the grass behind the busted water fountain, laughing.

It's only when I stop laughing that I realize how strange this is. Then I think the really strange thing is that it's strange. It used to be completely normal to be just mucking around and having a laugh, but now we never do it any more. With Carl, things aren't a laugh. He makes us do scary things, or exciting things, and sometimes we'll laugh at each other, but it's never like this, just playing and laughing.

When I look at Olly, I know he's thinking the same thing. And I know he isn't going to say anything about it.

Just at the moment when the feeling's about to snap, I say, 'Carl's a bit . . .' I can't think how I'm going to finish the sentence, and end up just saying, '. . . nuts.'

Olly shrugs.

'D'you ever think we were better off without him?' I say.

Olly stares at me. He doesn't move a muscle, but I can see he's fizzing inside.

It's a while before I realize what he's thinking. I know what he wants to say, and for a minute I can't figure out what's stopping him. Then it hits me that he thinks it might be a trap. He doesn't know if he should tell the truth because he thinks I might be asking so I can rat on him to Carl. It's incredible he could think this, but I can see it in his eyes. He's trying to figure out if he can trust me.

'I won't tell him!' I say, but it doesn't come out right. It's like I'm shouting at him.

'Tell him what you like,' he says. 'I'm not hiding anything.'

'I didn't say you were,' I say.

'Well, I'm not. He's my mate.'

'I know.'

'Why?' says Olly 'Are you saying you don't like him?'

'No.' It's not safe to tell the truth now. The moment's gone.

'So what are you talking about, then?'

'Nothing. I was just asking.'

'Asking what?'

'*Nothing*. Forget it.'

'Maybe I won't.'

'What's that supposed to mean?'

'Just that maybe I won't.'

'Won't what?'

'Won't forget what you said.'

'I didn't say anything.'

He raises an eyebrow at me, like he knows he's got one over on me, and walks off. I go after him, but don't say anything, and we get all the way back to his house in silence.

When he says bye, it sounds a bit like an apology, but I can't be sure. You can't tell where he stands any more. You don't really know what he's thinking.

the ironmonger's

I wouldn't say Carl's exactly scary. After the game of knuckles, he doesn't hit me once. But he doesn't have to. It's not like you can ever forget he's bigger.

He has a way now of heading off challenges before they even happen. If you say something he doesn't like, however small, he uses it against you, twisting it, going on and on about this tiny thing, bouncing it off the other person to grow it and mock you for it, and you can end up spending hours or even a whole day as the brunt of everything, just because of one little comment, so it becomes simpler to say only what you think he'll like. If you make things easier for him, you make things easier for yourself. That's just how it is.

But there's one day – a bunking day – when he turns up at McDonald's and he really is scary. He's all jumpy and his eyes are flashing, and he keeps standing up and checking himself in the mirrored wall, again and again, so many times that it begins to seem a bit crazy, and me and Olly have to pretend not to notice. There's something really hyper about the way he keeps smoothing the same bit of hair over and over. It reminds you of a zoo animal.

Neither of us wants to ask him if he's OK because we know he won't like it. For ages he doesn't say anything, and neither do we. Eventually he stops hopping around and stares at us – first me, then Olly, then me again.

'Let's steal a knife,' he says.

'A what?'

'A knife, you div. A knife and some rope.'

He's not joking. You can tell by the look on his face. I've never seen him more serious.

'Why?'

'There's something we have to do,' he says.

Then he stands and walks out. There's no option except to follow him.

'Robert Dyas – The Ironmonger', it says, which makes you think of an old man in front of an open fire, hammering out horse-shoes on an anvil, but it's nothing like that inside. It's just a big, deep old shop full of the kind of stuff that dads keep in sheds.

Carl's made a plan. Me and Olly are going to go in and buy some rope. He's already scouted it out and he says there's lots of different kinds, and we have to keep on asking to see all the different strengths until the shop guy is confused, and that's when Carl (who'll come in with us, but go straight to the back of the shop) will grab a knife and do a runner, preferably unnoticed. Even if they do notice him, he reckons he can run faster than them. And if he can't run faster than them, he'll have a knife and they won't. So nothing can go wrong.

He says if the shop guy asks why we want the rope, we should say it's a present for our dad. I'm not sure if that means we're pretending to be brothers, which I don't think will be very convincing, but it doesn't seem like that's an important question, so I don't bother him with it. He gives us fifteen quid, which he's got from I don't know where, to pay for the rope. He gets a bit aggressive when I ask how much rope he wants, and says he doesn't know, so I suggest we just get fifteen quids' worth, and he tells me to stop asking spastic questions because that's what the fifteen quid was for, so he doesn't know why I was even asking. It's unfair because he started off saying he didn't know, then ends up acting like I'm an idiot because *I* don't know. It was me that thought of the answer, not him. But things are often like that with Carl. He twists things round so it's always the other person who's the stupid one, and it's never worth arguing.

Strange thing is, the plan works. The old guy behind the counter gets so annoyed with us looking at all the different kinds of chains and ropes that he loses track of everything else, and a big queue builds up at the till, so the only other person in the shop has to come over and deal with it, and by the end there's so much bustle around us that even we don't know if Carl's got out all right. But he has.

Half an hour later, we're all in the park together, him with a long, serrated kitchen knife, us with about a ton of rope. Turns out fifteen quid goes a long way when you're buying rope.

When he sees it, Carl laughs at us and says we're idiots because we only need enough to tie up one person, but he never said that originally, so how were we supposed to know? Carl loves his knife, and for ages we chuck it around the park, seeing how many revolutions you can get it to do in the air and still land point downwards. Then we start just chucking it straight up, as high as we can, and running away to stop it landing on our heads, which is a good laugh.

It's Carl's idea to play chicken, where you stand with your legs apart and throw the knife into the grass between the other player's legs. You have to move your foot to where the knife went in, so with each round the gap gets smaller and smaller, and you end up aiming the knife at just a tiny piece of ground between the other person's feet.

We start with me v Carl, and when we're down to a gap of less than a hand I win because Carl misses and gets my shoe. It doesn't hurt too much but as winning prizes go, getting a knife in your foot isn't a great one. I only realize after I've won that it might have been better to lose. Olly says he doesn't fancy playing and, because it's Olly, Carl doesn't make him.

That's when I ask what the knife's for, and Carl tells us the plan.

'My dad lives in Swindon,' he says. 'I want to visit him. I have to show him something.'

'What? A knife?' I say.

'The knife's for his girlfriend.'

'Your dad's got a girlfriend?'

'I just said so, didn't I?'

'How come?'

'He ran off, didn't he. Years ago. Then he rings up Mum yesterday and tells her he's having a baby, in one month, with the girlfriend in Swindon, and he wants a proper divorce.'

'So what are you going to do?'

'I'm going to get her.'

'Get her?'

'She can't just take him. We've got to show her.'

'Show her what?'

'Teach her a lesson. Cut out her baby.'

'You're going to *cut out her baby*?'

'Don't be stupid. I'm just going to scare her. That's what we're going to do. All of us. We're going to go up there and scare her. Let her know she can't smash up my family.'

'How?'

'I'll work it all out.'

'What do we have to do?'

'Are you too chicken? Are you saying you're too chicken?' He stares at us, his eyes going from one to the other, pinning us back with their glare.

Olly shakes his head first, then me. There isn't any way out of it. Neither of us contradicts Carl any more, and now would be the stupidest time to start, with him looking more scary and serious than ever. We don't have any choice.

By now my foot's tingling, and there's a bubble of blood coming up inside one of my shoelace eyelets, so I tell them I'm going home. Carl says we have to divvy up the stuff for our trip. He's going to take the knife, and Olly, he says, can have the rope. He cuts off the length we'll need, sawing at it while me and Olly hold it taut, like a mini tug-of-war, then he chucks the rest into a bush.

It makes me feel wary, being left out like that while Olly gets to look after the rope. It means I'm the one he trusts least.

'What about me?' I say.

'What *about* you?' he says.

'What am I in charge of?'

He thinks for a bit, then says, 'Tape.'

'What kind of tape?'

'Like in films. For putting over someone's mouth. To stop them speaking.'

'The stuff for parcels?'

'Yeah. You got any? In your house?'

'Probably.'

'Well, you can bring that.'

'Bring it where?'

'To do the thing.'

'When?'

'Dunno. Next week.' Then he sees that Olly's got the rope

wound into a loop and slung over his shoulder. 'In your bag, you div! You've got to hide it!' he snaps, shoving him in the chest.

'I know!' says Olly, even though he didn't.

There's not much to say as we all walk home. Having a secret makes it hard to talk about anything else that isn't secret. Neither of them notice I'm limping.

As we shuffle along, I try and figure out if Carl really means it about the plan. It could be like the Wembley trip again, but further, and better. It could be fun, the three of us, going somewhere together, on a mission. I know it won't be, though. Not with Carl acting strange and taking funny equipment. It really won't be fun.

I don't want to go. I don't want to be his friend. I want to tell Mum that Carl's got a knife and is talking about using it.

I couldn't, though. He'd kill me.

the bathroom

I forget to lock the bathroom door. I wouldn't normally be that stupid. It must be the pain in my foot, from where Carl's knife got me. Donny walks in just as I'm trying to put a plaster on. I haven't even started getting the blood off my shoe and sock yet, so the evidence is right there for him to see.

He's got a sixth sense for when I want to be left alone, and that's when he comes and finds me.

'What are you doing?' he says.

'Hurt my foot.'

'How?'

I shrug. 'Just hurt it.'

'What were you doing?'

'Nothing.'

'You were doing nothing, and your foot just sprang a leak?'

'LEAVE ME ALONE!' It's at the top of my voice. I didn't even know I could shout that loud.

Donny stares at me, like he thinks I'm crazy. 'Are you OK?' he says.

'LEAVE ME ALONE! LEAVE ME ALONE!' Even though I'm shouting, I'm hoping he won't do it.

For ages he doesn't speak, then he says, 'It was Carl, wasn't it? Show me.' He tries to pull my hands away from where they're hiding my foot, but I tense up and don't let him. He's too strong, though, and I can only hold it for a few seconds. Once he's prised my grip loose, I give up and let him look.

Donny stares at the cut, thinking.

'Was this a knife?'

'It was an accident. We were playing a game.'

'I'm going to have to tell Mum and Dad.'

'DON'T!'

'I have to. You've been cu –'

'DON'T TELL THEM! THEY WON'T UNDERSTAND!'

'*I* don't understand,' he says.

'Yes, you do. It's just games. Just stupid games. Sometimes they go wrong.'

'It's not normal, what he does to you. It's not safe. You have to stay away from him.'

'I CAN'T.'

'You have to.'

'I CAN'T.'

'Why not?'

'Because.'

'Because what?'

'Because he's my friend. Him and Olly are my friends.'

'So get new friends. Get friends who are nice to you.'

'I can't!'

'You can.'

'I can't. You can't just change friends. It doesn't work. I tried, and it doesn't work.'

'It takes time, but you can do it. You have to.'

'IT DOESN'T WORK! IT DOESN'T WORK! YOU DON'T UNDER-STAND!'

'I do understand.'

'You don't. You don't know what it's like.'

'What what's like?'

'See? You *don't* understand.'

'Ben – listen. I'll do a deal with you. I won't tell anyone about this if you make me a promise. If you promise, on your life, that you won't see Carl again, and that you'll try, properly, to change friends, I'll keep quiet. OK? If you see him once more, I'm telling Mum and Dad.'

He's got me cornered. I can't have them knowing. They'd start prying into school stuff and might find out about the bunking, then that would be the end of everything. I have to make the promise. It's only words, after all. They don't really mean anything. They're just what I've got to say to stop my world falling apart. He can't make me mean it, and he can't make me do it. I'm not going back to Blob. There's no way I'll ever let myself become a nobody again.

I nod.

'Say it,' he says.

'I promise.'

'Promise what?' he says.

'To not see Carl.'

'Say the whole thing.'

'I promise not to see Carl.'

'And look at me while you're saying it.'

'IpromisenottoseeCarl!'

'Good.'

He stares at me for a bit, then turns and leaves.

From the corridor, just his head peeking back into the room, he tells me not to be an idiot, and that he's going to keep an eye on me.

I kick the door shut, which makes the cut zap me right up the leg.

the station

It's Wednesday, a week later, that Carl sets as the big day. He's got money for train tickets from somewhere, and he's figured out how to catch a Swindon train, and he seems to know everything. Sometimes he seems stupid, but often I think he might be the cleverest of any of us.

The plan is that we're going to meet at the Tube station at nine. Carl will have the knife, Olly the rope, and me the tape. We'll get the Tube into London, then change on to an intercity that goes to Swindon. After that it's all just in Carl's head. He says he knows what to do, and he'll tell us as we go along.

It's not like we discuss it. There's never even a moment when he asks if we want to go. He just tells us the plan – what bits we're allowed to know – and we do as he says.

I'm scared of going, but I'm more scared of not going. I'm in Carl's gang now and, once you're in, you can't pick and choose what you're up for. You're all in or all out. I made my choice when I went back to him. If I don't turn up, or tell on him, he'll get his revenge. Whatever you do to Carl, he does back to you, twice as bad. It's never worth it. I have to go.

Everyone in the world except us three thinks it's just an ordinary school day. No one knows that the three of us are on a mission to beat all missions. I'm so nervous about it that over breakfast Mum even asks me if something's wrong. I just tell her I'm late, and rush upstairs to do my teeth. I don't want her looking at me too hard in case she figures something out. You can never tell how much of what you're thinking is showing when it's Mum that's looking at you.

Then I set off without the tape. It's all I have to remember, but my head's so buzzy I forget all about it until I've got to the end of the road, at the corner where I should be going left, to school, but aren't. Carl will kill me if I turn up without the one thing that was my job. I have to go back.

It's going to be ten times harder to smuggle the tape out of the house now because if anyone sees me they're going to ask why I've come home again, and I'll have to make up an excuse, but I don't have a choice. It's my own fault.

I open the door extra quietly, pulling it towards me so the latch doesn't click. From the hall I can hear Mum upstairs getting ready for work. The tape's in the cupboard under the sink. Thinking I might be able to get in and out of the house without anyone noticing, I slip into the kitchen, but Donny's there, eating his breakfast.

He looks funny when he's just got up, Donny. Everything's squished and rumpled and puffy, so badly you'd think a dog's slept on his head. It takes about two hours before you see his eyes. For speech, anything more than a grunt is a miracle. So even though he's right there, munching through his cereal, there's still a chance I might be able to walk right past him, fetch the tape and leave, without Donny looking up.

I get all the way to the sink without him seeming to notice I'm even in the room. I fish out the tape, quietly but casually, and stroll back in the least hurried way I can manage. I've got one foot into the hallway when Donny says, 'What are you doing?' His face is still down over his cereal. You'd think he was speaking to the Sugar Puffs.

'Going to school.'

He looks up at me. 'Twice?' he says.

'Forgot something.'

'Packing tape?'

It's right there, in my hand. I can't deny it. 'Yeah.'

'Why are you taking packing tape to school?'

'For a project.'

'On what?'

'Er . . . parcels.'

I'm not sounding very convincing, so I decide to just run for it.

I've got the front door halfway open when Donny's foot kicks it shut. He stands there in front of me, blocking the way. He doesn't say anything, he just stares down at me. I don't look up. I stay still, looking at the door, breathing heavily, waiting for him to let me through.

'What are you doing, Ben?' he says.

'Nothing.'

'Tell me what you're doing.'

'I'm going to school! Let me go!'

'We've got a deal, Ben.'

'Let me go! I'm late!'

'Late for school?'

'Yes!'

'For your project on parcels?'

'LEAVE ME ALONE! LEAVE ME ALONE!'

I kick him, hard as I can, on the shin. He yelps and loses his balance. I push him out of the way and, in a flash, I'm out of the door and down the street.

I'm supposed to be at the station by now, but I don't want to run and look all flustered when I arrive. One of the most important things in the whole plan, Carl said, was that we look natural all day and don't draw attention to ourselves. So I walk it. It's the fastest walk I can manage, but it's still a walk. Part of the plan for looking normal was that we'd all go there on our own.

The station's about ten minutes away at the bottom of a cul-de-sac. When I get there, from the end of the street I see Carl and Olly, waiting for me under the station awning, next to one another, standing close, but not talking. There's a bush on the corner, and even though I'm late, even though I've been rushing all the way from home, I stand there, hidden behind the leaves, watching them.

It feels like that moment on the way to Wembley, when Carl had crossed over Kenton Road, almost getting hit, and I was still on the other side, watching him through the traffic. I get the same feeling I had then – that I'm in one world and Carl's in another.

I stare at them, my legs suddenly refusing to carry me any further because I know this is my last chance. If I go down there and get on a train with them, Carl's going to take us somewhere new. Somewhere bad. Somewhere me and Olly can't even imagine.

Carl's looking right at the bush now, staring in my direction, and I begin to think maybe he can see me there, maybe I'm not properly hidden, maybe he knows I'm having doubts. It's so stupid of me to leave it until now before really thinking about what I'm getting involved in because just by being here, to meet them, just by agreeing to the whole thing in advance, I've already left it too late to back out. Carl always makes it seem like you don't have a choice.

Then a hand grabs my shoulder and pulls me back round the

corner. The fright of it feels like an electric shock ripping right through me, rattling my heart and fizzing my veins. My throat constricts to form a scream, just as I see who it is.

Donny. He's still wearing pyjamas. He's got one of Dad's big coats over the top, and his feet are slipped into a pair of trainers. He's out of breath from running.

'Where are you going?' he says.

I can't answer.

'Tell me where you're going.'

I can't even look at him. My mouth's clamped shut and my eyes are down to the pavement. My chest's rising and falling, fighting for air, and my heart's beating so loud I can hear it in my ears.

Suddenly I'm in mid air. Donny's yanked me up and pinned me against a fence. He leans in to me, nose to nose, so I can't not look at him.

'What are you doing, Ben? What are you doing?'

'Nothing.'

'THAT'S NOT GOOD ENOUGH, BEN! TELL ME!'

With my shirt cutting into both armpits, and Donny staring me down, his hands jabbed against my throat, and knowing that Carl's just round the corner, waiting, it all becomes too much, and I can't hold in the tears any longer. It's just an itch in the eyes at first, and a tingling at the end of my nose, but as soon as it happens I know I'm not going to be able to stop it. By the way Donny looks at me I can tell he knows, too, and he puts me down, but even though I'm welling up, I can still see the sad way he looks at me, and I can still see what's coming up behind him.

'DONNYYYYYY!!!!'

The second I shout it, he swivels round. Right there, just a couple of steps away, is Carl, arm out, knife pointed straight at my brother's chest. Just behind him is Olly.

Holding the knife steady, Carl flicks his eyes between Donny and me, his knees slightly bent, ready to lunge.

'Why d'you bring him?' says Carl, and you can tell by his voice he's angry enough to totally lose control.

'I didn't!' I say.

'WHY D'YOU BRING HIM?'

'I DIDN'T! HE FOLLOWED ME! I DIDN'T KNOW ANYTHING ABOUT IT!'

'Why'd he follow you?'

'I don't know.'

'WHY?'

'I DON'T KNOW! ASK HIM!'

Carl turns to Donny, and they stare at one another, the knife glinting in the space between them.

'Why'd you follow him?' says Carl.

'What do you want with my brother?' says Donny. 'Why can't you just leave him alone?'

'I'M ASKING THE QUESTIONS!' Carl shouts. It sounds odd, the way he says it. You can tell it's a line he's heard on telly.

There's a long silence while Carl looks from Donny to me and back again, and Donny stares from the knife to Carl. By Donny's face, I can see he's figuring something out – making a calculation.

'Come on,' says Donny. 'We're going home.'

With that, he turns round and reaches a hand towards mine. At first sight, it's crazy. He's just standing there now, with his back to Carl and the knife, defenceless. Carl could stab him in an instant, but Donny's doing nothing about it. He's not even acting like he's scared. His body looks relaxed and slow.

I'm the only one that can see his face, though, and from the clench of his jaw and the tightness over his eyes, it's obvious he's afraid. He looks right into my eyes, and I suddenly understand what he's doing. He isn't just grabbing me and running off. His hand has stopped short of mine so I have to decide what to do. I have to reach out and take it.

It's my choice. Between him and Carl. And every second I wait is a second he has to spend with his back to Carl and the knife.

As soon as I understand, I take his hand.

I'm expecting him to grab it and run, but he doesn't. He just slips his fingers round my palm, gives me an extra little squeeze for courage and, without turning, or saying anything, or hurrying, the two of us walk away, showing the full stretch of both backs to Carl.

As we take our first few steps I can hear the stillness behind us. I want to turn and check that Carl's not coming after us – I want to see what look there is on his face – but I know I have to just do what Donny's doing. He's in charge now.

I hear a faint rumbling from up by the station.

'It's the train, Carl,' Olly says. 'It's the train.'

I can hear that Carl still hasn't moved. I can sense his mind whirring, deciding what to do to us, with the train arriving behind him, us walking away in front of him, and the knife still gripped in his hand.

Then there's the sudden scuffing of trainers against pavement and the sound of four feet sprinting. Sprinting away. They've run for the train.

Once they're gone – once I've heard the train come and go, and looked round to check they haven't come back out of the station – all the blood drains from my legs, and the plug finally comes out on my tears. I sob like a baby, so hard I can barely stand, and Donny scoops me up, puts me on his back and carries me home.

We must look a weird sight, Donny in his pyjamas and an overcoat, giving his little brother a piggyback across Kenton Road in the middle of the morning rush hour. People probably stare. But I don't notice anything. My eyes are shut, and I feel nothing except the sobs jerking my body, and my brother's arms firmly around my legs, holding my weight, carrying me home.

here, now

That's why you'd never heard of me. It's only thanks to Donny. I don't think things would have gone as far as they did with me there, but I would have been in on it, and it wouldn't have been 'Carl Murray and Oliver Ward – The Two Evil Boys', it would have been three of us.

They're famous now, Carl and Olly. Someone told me even people in China have heard of them. The newspapers never wrote about me. People didn't know I was nearly involved unless they were at my school or from my street.

Some people said Donny should have called the police and got the boys stopped before they arrived, but that was my fault, too. I made him promise not to tell anyone. I said we had to save the police as a threat. I thought Carl would return from the trip wanting to get his own back. I never knew he wouldn't return at all. And I never knew what he was going to do. I thought he was just going to scare her.

Donny took the blame for not calling the police. He never told anyone I wouldn't let him. It's thanks to Donny that all I got was you. You're my punishment. Carl and Olly got borstal. I got a social worker. I got you – you and your boring, boring visits.

People changed after it happened. Once word got round, every-one wanted a good look, wanted to know who I was, but no one would talk to me. At school, everyone avoided me, even

Blob. The teachers were kind, but in a nosy, curious way, and I could tell they secretly hated me. Mrs Sparks locked her gate, so I couldn't get balls out of her garden any more.

After a while we moved house, to where people didn't know who I was.

On the day we left, Lucy came round, and the way Rachel looked at her when she appeared from behind the removal van was like something in a cowboy film. I thought Rachel was going to draw a gun and shoot her, but she didn't.

They only talked for a few minutes, but it must have made a difference because now Rachel gets a letter from her almost every day. Rachel must write back, but that's the kind of thing you're not allowed to see or discuss or know about.

She listens to drony music instead of thumpy music these days, but I think she likes it here. She goes out again now, like a normal person. Donny hates it, but he's leaving home soon. Our new garden's like a jungle, so Dad's happy, always out there with his tools, chopping things down and digging things up. He says he'll make it so there's space for football, but I'm not bothered.

Everyone's different now, even Mum. She often looks at me in the way you'd stare into a well, trying to see what's down there. I never did anything bad to anyone, but just because I was Carl and Olly's friend people think I'm partly to blame. She never says it, no one ever does, but sometimes I know even my own mum's thinking it.

Acknowledgements

Thanks to Maggie O'Farrell, Felicity Rubinstein, Tony Lacey, Sarah Lutyens, Brian Rea, Zelda Turner, Susannah Godman, Helen Fraser, Richard Sved, Kate Webb, Saul Venit, Alex Garland, Matthew Sweet and John, Sue and Adam Sutcliffe.